Taking Flight

by

Kate Randle

Taking Flight

Cover Art by *Kristian Norris*

The Wild Rose Press, Inc.
PO Box 708
Adams Basin, NY 14410-0708
Visit us at www.thewildrosepress.com

Publishing History
First Champagne Rose Edition, 2017
Print ISBN 978-1-5092-1603-1
Digital ISBN 978-1-5092-1604-8

Published in the United States of America

Dedication

I dedicate this novel
to my wonderful husband, Jason,
and my two children.
At every twist and turn in this amazing journey,
they have helped me make my dreams come true.

Acknowledgments

I would like to thank my editor, Sherri Good, for the wonderful job she did to help me make this novel the best it could be. And a big thank-you goes out to Joyce Mochrie for taking one last look.

And to my readers, thank you for picking up this copy of *Taking Flight*. I hope Lucas and Ivy's story touches your heart as much as it did mine.

Chapter One

A familiar feeling of dread crept over Ivy Castlefield as she made her way toward the gate. She had always hated flying, despite the fact she had done it with alarming regularity for her entire career. But this was the first flight she had taken in six months, so the fear had been given a chance to take root in her once again.

The airport was busy this first Sunday morning in December, bustling with people going here and there. The noise of the crowd was a low hum, and the speakers made announcements every few minutes warning passengers not to leave their bags unattended. John F. Kennedy Airport in New York City was one of the largest, but she knew it well.

She had arrived by taxi from her loft apartment on the Upper East Side three hours before her flight. Checking in with the airline went smoothly, and she breezed through security without any problems. Now all she wanted to do was grab her morning caffeine fix and find a seat to wait for her boarding call. She could smell the freshly brewed coffee and muffins from the local bakery as she passed by.

At five-foot-eight, Ivy looked over the heads of many of the passengers as she weaved her way slowly through the crowd. This trip she was taking to Las Vegas was designed to help her cope with recent events by allowing her to move on with her life. She needed to get back to work, and this conference was an opportunity to prove it to herself. At least that's what her agent had convinced her of. To be honest, she wasn't entirely sure about the whole thing, but sitting around her apartment for the past few months had been not only depressing but very unproductive.

She spied her gate and calculated she had twenty minutes to kill before her flight would begin boarding. Making her way over to the coffee shop, she ordered an extra-large with cream and sugar. Then she found a seat near her gate and sat down to enjoy the fragrant brew. The coffee was hot and strong, just how she liked it.

She savored every sip as she watched the people around her come and go. Many were in a hurry, and more than a few were stressed out. Some families with small children struggled to feed and entertain their little ones while they waited for their flights. She always thought she would have had children by now, but life had a cruel way of throwing her curveballs when she least expected it.

The loudspeaker blared to life, knocking Ivy out of her wayward thoughts and into the present moment. Her flight was ready to board. Since she was booked in First Class, her section boarded first. She lined up with businessmen and a few senior citizens and waited for the attendants to check boarding passes. Taking a few deep breaths, she tried to calm herself down.

The airport worker checked her ticket without comment and ushered her down the long hallway to board the plane. She found her window seat, stowed her briefcase in the overhead bin, and was relieved to see that no one was sitting beside her. Ivy didn't feel like small talk. She retrieved her tablet from her bag before she settled into the comfortable leather seat. There was a lot of work for her to do before the conference tomorrow, and although she was normally prepared well in advance for these things, that was not the case with this trip.

Her carefully organized and confident persona had somehow slipped away from her. It felt like a lifetime ago since she had been a successful motivational speaker and happily married to the love of her life. Now she was still a motivational speaker on paper, but she hadn't presented anywhere in months. And even though her most recent book remained on the bestseller list, it wouldn't stay there forever.

Her agent had finally come to her apartment to see her and give her an ultimatum. Get back in the game or risk her entire career she had worked so hard to build. She heeded his warning, but right now, she wasn't so sure that had been the best decision.

Unfortunately, it was too late for thoughts like that. She was booked to speak at a two-day conference for an audience of the most elite information technology leaders in the country, and she had no idea what she was going to say to them. Well, she'd better think of something—fast. Ivy distracted herself by turning on her tablet and opening the files of her past speeches. She could just take the easy way out and use one of them, but that wasn't her style.

Ivy wanted to bring a fresh voice to every speaking engagement, and although her message was often the same, she felt energized by presenting the material in new and exciting ways. If only she could get back some of those optimistic feelings that were buried with her late husband six months earlier.

She sighed and settled in for the almost six-hour flight, surely enough time to come up with a half-decent one-hour speech. It looked like everyone had boarded, and the flight attendants were demonstrating the safety features of the aircraft as it taxied out to the runway. Ivy tried to pay attention, but she had seen this presentation so many times, she thought she could repeat it in her sleep. Once the flight attendants took their seats, the pilot's voice flowed from the loudspeaker to welcome the passengers.

"Good Morning." The deep sexy sound got Ivy's attention immediately. "I'm Captain Lucas Freeman, and my co-pilot is Ben McIntyre. On behalf of myself and the flight crew, we would like to welcome you aboard Fantasy Flight 2375 which is non-stop to McCarran International Airport in Las Vegas."

Ivy felt like she could listen to this man talk for hours, if not days. She hadn't heard a voice this smooth since she was addicted to talk radio in her late teens and early twenties. But surely it could not belong to a man as good-looking as she imagined. No, he was probably middle-aged and balding with a hideous moustache. But still, she kept listening.

"Our flying time is five hours and fifty-five minutes at a cruising altitude of thirty-five thousand feet. The weather in Las Vegas is partly sunny and sixty-eight degrees. We are next in line for takeoff. Enjoy your flight."

And with that said, he clicked off the speaker, and the plane veered toward the runway. Ivy leaned back in her seat and closed her eyes. She hated the takeoff and landing part the most, although the pilot's voice had a somewhat calming effect on her. It was weird, and she couldn't explain it, but it was what it was.

A few minutes later, the plane left the ground, and Ivy breathed a sigh of relief. The flight attendants came around and offered breakfast and drinks to the passengers, but Ivy just ordered an orange juice. She didn't eat when she was flying. Her stomach was queasy enough.

After she was served, she went hard to work on her speech. Ivy was so engrossed, a whole hour had gone by before she even realized the time. She didn't notice someone had sat down beside her until he spoke.

"Excuse me, Ms. Castlefield," said that smooth, sexy voice she had heard before take off. She thought she must be imagining things. Then she glanced up and saw him.

She was looking into the most exquisite green eyes she had ever seen, and the face surrounding them was unbelievably handsome. Strong cheekbones and a chiseled jaw stood out beneath naturally tanned skin. His hair was light brown and longish with golden streaks in it, like he spent a lot of time in the sun. He had a neatly trimmed goatee in the same shade as his hair. His breathtaking smile faltered as he looked at her. She needed to say something, but what?

"Hello," she managed, tearing her eyes away from his and feeling her cheeks flush with embarrassment. *What is the pilot doing here, sitting beside her in the vacant seat?* He was dressed in a crisp, white shirt with gold and black epaulets emblazoned on his broad shoulders.

Ivy felt underdressed in her yoga pants and sweater now that she was faced with this gorgeous man in uniform. But he didn't seem to notice. She had no idea what to say to him. Fortunately, he broke the silence.

"I wanted to welcome you onboard Fantasy Airlines and ask if you were having an enjoyable flight today."

"Um, yes, thank you, Captain…"

"Please, call me Lucas."

"Okay, Lucas." To call the captain by his first name was way too informal for her, yet she did it anyway. "Yes, thank you. The flight has been great so far."

"Good," he said, smiling that stunning smile again. "I have to say I wanted to meet you as soon as I saw your name on the passenger manifest. You're an inspiring speaker, and I follow your work. I attended your presentation to airport personnel in Miami last year, but I didn't get a chance to meet you."

"Why thank you," Ivy said. She didn't feel like an inspirational speaker right now. She was perfectly tongue-tied in front of this handsome stranger. Fortunately, he had more to say.

"So I wanted to say hello to you and introduce myself. Please let me or the crew know if you need anything for the duration of your flight."

He stood up and held out a hand for her to shake. When their skin made contact, Ivy felt a surge of passion rise up in her, the likes of which she had never felt before. His large hand was warm and comforting wrapped around her small one. She fantasized for a moment what it would feel like to have his strong, muscular arms wrapped around her. Then she felt her face flush with heat as she shook her head to clear her thoughts.

"Thank you again," she finally said. "And it was very nice to meet you, too."

He smiled one more time and then disappeared back into the cockpit. Ivy leaned back in her seat. Wow. He was the most handsome pilot she had ever laid eyes on. And that voice. He appeared to want to say more to her, but she couldn't put her finger on exactly what. Did he want to ask her out? No, that couldn't be it. She was a widow for goodness sake.

And then guilt overwhelmed her like she was somehow betraying her late husband by talking to another man. However, before Matt had died—in one of his more lucid moments—he made her promise she wouldn't live the rest of her life reliving memories of the past. She promised him she would move on, but it was easier said than done. Besides, it was too soon. Anyway, she was probably imagining Lucas's attraction to her. Five months living alone in an apartment was bound to make a person a bit crazy. She blew out a long breath and got back to work.

****

Lucas made his way back to the pilot's seat and sighed. He had made a complete fool of himself by saying hello to Ivy Castlefield. That woman was way out of his league. He thought the fact he was a pilot might impress her, but she was probably used to millionaire bankers asking her out, and he was small potatoes in comparison to that. She was, by far, the most gorgeous woman he had ever seen. Her white-blonde hair was naturally beautiful and those eyes. He could get lost in their violet-blue depths. *Well, I hope you took a good look because I'm pretty sure she never wants to see your face again.*

With a grim expression, he reentered the front of the plane. The look on his face when he entered the cockpit made his co-pilot, Ben, burst out laughing. "Oh no," he said. "Did the handsome and dashing Lucas Freeman strike out with the beautiful Ivy Castlefield?"

"Shut up," Lucas replied and smiled at his coworker and friend. "Or I'll fire you."

"Sure, sure. You couldn't live without me, and you know it."

"Well, I'm stuck with you for the duration of this flight at least, and then we shall see."

"Okay, but seriously, what happened?"

"Well, I said hello, but that was about it. She's enchanting and gorgeous, but she seemed a little distant. I wanted to say more, but then I just didn't."

Ben gave Lucas a playful slap on the shoulder. "Don't worry about it, buddy. I'm sure she'll be knocking on the cockpit door by the end of the flight, begging for your phone number."

"I doubt it," Lucas replied. "But thanks. Now, what did I miss here?"

"Well, I didn't want to disturb you on your date, but the weather over Nebraska isn't looking promising—thunderstorms and high winds. What do you want to do?"

This was not good. He didn't need this today. "Can we change course?"

"Negative. There are too many planes in the airspace if we try to go around it. We are going to have to go through it. Are you ready?"

"Yes, but it's not going to be pretty. Go alert the flight attendants and instruct them to have the passengers stay in their seats. This plane ride is about to get very bumpy."

"Okay, ten-four, Captain. I'll get right on it."

Lucas sat down at the controls while Ben went to alert the other staff. A rocky flight was something he hadn't anticipated. He had been working non-stop the entire month, and he was tired—really tired. But he was an experienced pilot and could handle whatever was thrown at him.

At thirty-two years old, he had been flying commercial planes for over five years now. His love of flying had started in his teens and never stopped. Unlike all his other high school peers, he knew exactly what he wanted to do for a career and began planning it all out in the ninth grade. Looking back, he somehow felt like he missed out on a lot of things other young people did—like dating, for instance—but it didn't bother him until recent months.

Now, so many of his friends were getting married and settling down, and he was becoming known as the perpetual bachelor. He didn't really have the outgoing, carefree personality that normally went with the dating scene, so he had thrown himself into his work instead. Despite this, he couldn't really get the stunning Ivy out of his mind.

Once he dealt with this latest weather crisis, maybe he would go back and talk to her again—maybe ask her out on a date. What did he have to lose? Besides, if she said no, he'd never see her again, and then he could just forget the whole thing. It was something to think about, that was after he got this plane through the impending storm.

****

Ivy was fidgeting in her seat. Being unable to sit

still or get up and walk around the cabin was making her half crazy. The flight attendants hadn't said much, but the seat belt sign was turned on, and the passengers were asked to stay put due to the turbulence they would soon be experiencing. Once again, she chided herself for agreeing to this trip. If she had said no, she'd be safely stowed away in her apartment right now, doing what, exactly? Well, she wasn't sure, but anything was better than this.

Her fear of flying always came back to haunt her when the plane ride became bumpy. Even the flight attendants were fastened safely in their seats, so she couldn't order a glass of alcohol which she needed to soothe her frayed nerves. She tried some deep-breathing exercises she had learned in her yoga class, but they weren't helping very much. Closing the speech she had been working on, she put on her headphones and tried to listen to the soothing sounds of nature. When that didn't work, she almost cried out in frustration—but then the loudspeaker blared to life once again.

"Ladies and gentlemen. Thank you for your patience with us during this difficult flight."

Why did she instantly feel relaxed at the sound of his voice? He must have this effect on all women, she mused. Nevertheless, she felt calm, despite the fact the plane ride continued to be rocky. She closed her eyes and listened.

"We are experiencing some more-than-normal turbulence during this flight. Unfortunately, due to more upcoming thunderstorms that can't be avoided, we have to make an emergency landing in Denver. Once the weather clears, you will be put on another flight to your final destination. We apologize for the inconvenience and will be providing all passengers with hotel accommodations and an additional free flight anywhere Fantasy Airlines travels to. Once again, thank you."

He clicked off the loudspeaker, and Ivy let out a sigh she didn't realize she had been holding. A delay? A stopover in Denver? This she didn't need. She wasn't presenting at the conference until Tuesday, but she wanted to attend the event tomorrow to get a feel for the crowd. Now she thought she would be lucky if she made it on time for her speech.

The other passengers around her were grumbling about the delay, but unlike her, they were all very vocal. Ivy couldn't help but feel sorry for Lucas. She thought he was a nice guy and didn't deserve the nasty things the passengers were saying. Would they rather have him push through the storm and risk a crash? No one wanted that, but most people only cared about themselves and their priorities. And since this was a big inconvenience, as the pilot, he was the natural one to blame.

Despite this, she didn't feel like that. She flashed back to their brief meeting: his commanding presence in his crisp uniform, his kind smile, beautiful eyes, and hair she could imagine herself running her hands through. Then she thought for a moment about what it would be like to go out with a man like Lucas Freeman. What was she thinking? Now she really was going crazy.

He wasn't interested in her like that. Sure, he liked her work, but that didn't translate into having a personal interest in her. Besides, she was a widow, and that, in itself, was unattractive. She might as well take up knitting and get five cats because she was destined to become a spinster.

The plane suddenly descended, and Ivy gripped her armrests. When this plane got on the ground, the first thing she was going to do was grab a nice stiff drink.

****

After another grueling hour at the controls, Lucas got the plane on the ground in Denver. It had been touch and go. They were dodging lightning and high winds—which made the control of the plane very difficult—but he'd managed to do it like the professional he was. Now, as he was seated in the bar of the airport hotel, he could relax for a few hours. He wouldn't be flying until tomorrow at the earliest, so he ordered another scotch on the rocks.

His co-pilot and best friend, Ben, had deserted him a half hour before, saying he could no longer keep his eyes open after the two beers he had consumed. Lucas himself was too wired to sleep. The bar was quiet at this hour. He assumed most people would be ordering a late lunch or early dinner at this time of day, not alcoholic beverages. Well, he didn't follow the schedule of most people, so here he was.

He looked around the nicely appointed space. The bar and surrounding furnishings were done in a dark wood. Glasses lined the area above his head, and the back of the bar was stocked with various high-quality spirits. The lighting was dim—which was soothing to his tired eyes—and the plush navy blue carpeting kept the noise to a minimum.

The bartender was friendly but mostly left Lucas alone with his thoughts. He wasn't a big conversationalist on the best of days, and this was not one of his better days. It was true he had saved the lives of many people today due to his skills as a pilot, however, most of his efforts went unappreciated in the commercial airline business. Some of his friends had encouraged him to become a private pilot, but he didn't want to be at the beck and call of one customer. It wasn't his style.

Dressed casually in dark jeans and a black sweater, he no longer looked like a pilot and that suited him just fine. He had experienced enough of that for one day. Lucas was just a guy drinking in a bar, like any other person in here. Then a familiar voice roused him from his thoughts.

"Excuse me, is this seat taken?"

Lucas looked up from his drink. Staring back at him was the exquisite Ivy Castlefield. She was smiling at him this time, and she was even more beautiful than ever before. Her hair was pulled back into a bun, and her eyes were shining with dark mischief. She was dressed casually in yoga pants and a gray sweater, but now that she was standing, he could see the outfit hugged her curves in all the right places.

"Hi," he said, finding his voice again. She was the last person he expected to see here, so to say he was taken by surprise would be an understatement. With the stress of landing the plane and making sure all the passengers got off safely, he had forgotten his promise to himself to go back and talk to her. And now, here she was. "Please sit down, Ivy. May I call you that?"

"Of course," she said, taking a seat beside him. "What are you drinking, Captain?"

"Scotch on the rocks. Would you like one after that disastrous flight?"

"Well, I'm more of a wine girl. And I wouldn't call the flight a disaster. We're still here, aren't we? It could have been much worse. But still, could I have a glass of white?"

"Sure thing," he said and signaled the bartender. When he had given her drink order, he turned back to her.

"Tell me the truth. What were the other passengers really saying about me when I was trying to avert disaster?"

"Well, let's just say most of them were self-absorbed and leave it at that. But this passenger thought you did a great job."

"Really?"

The bartender set down a glass of white wine in front of Ivy and sauntered away.

She nodded at him. "Yes, and take it from a frequent flyer. You handled that plane the best way you could. Very professional."

"Thank you. I don't get too many compliments in this industry, so that means a lot."

"You're very welcome. And there's something else."

"What is it?" He was enjoying talking to this beautiful woman, and his fatigue was long forgotten as he focused on her violet-blue eyes.

"I'm sorry we kind of got off on the wrong foot when you introduced yourself on the plane."

He was taken aback by her comment, although truth be told, he was the one who had acted strangely when they first met. He had been somewhat starstruck, and she was infinitely more striking in person than the photo on the back of her book jacket. He thought for a second. "Well, you did seem a bit distant, but I get it. You're a big celebrity and don't want to be bothered. I think I may have overstepped a boundary by approaching you. I'm sorry for that."

She shook her head. "No, it's not that at all. To be honest, I don't consider myself a celebrity, and I'm flattered you like my work. It's just that I'm terrified of flying. I get really closed off on flights so I won't freak out the other passengers or myself."

"C'mon, is that true?" Since he loved it with all his heart and soul, it was hard for him to imagine someone not liking to fly, although he had seen his share of frightened passengers during his time as a pilot. "I don't believe it. Besides, you must fly all the time for your career. Aren't you used to it by now?"

"Yes and no. Hey, take my word for it, okay? I'm just glad I got a chance to meet you again and explain everything. I wouldn't want you to think I was weird or anything."

"Trust me; I don't think you're weird. But as a pilot, you know I love to fly, so I don't understand that part. But maybe we could discuss it further. Would you like to order some food with your wine?" He held up the bar menu he had been perusing earlier. He'd thought about ordering some lunch, but he hated to eat alone so he had set the menu aside. Now, faced with this enchanting woman, his appetite was back with a vengeance.

She smiled at him. This day had started out as a big disaster, but things were looking up.

"Sure," she said and took the menu he was holding out. "I don't eat before I fly, so to be honest, I'm starving."

"Wonderful. I am, too. Order whatever you'd like; it's on me."

"Thank you," she replied. "That's very sweet."

"It's the least I can do for stranding you in a strange city, nowhere near your destination. By the way, what's in Las Vegas?"

"Oh, I'm giving a speech at a conference on Tuesday."

"That's great. I'd heard you weren't presenting after...well, that's none of my business..." He shouldn't have brought up what the news had to say about her personal life. He expected her to look at him with disgust and walk out of the bar, but instead, she just nodded.

"No, it's okay. Yeah, I've been going through a rough patch these last few months, but I think I'm ready to get back into it."

Lucas held up his hands. "Look, I'm sorry. You don't owe me an explanation about anything."

"It's fine, really. Besides, it helps to talk about it one-on-one. I'm going to get bombarded at the conference, so I need to be prepared."

"Well then, tell me, Ivy Castlefield, where have you been hiding for the last five months?"

She smiled at his comment. "Unfortunately, it's not nearly as glamorous as it sounds. I've mostly been alone in my apartment, trying to figure out how a motivational speaker goes on after tragedy strikes her life. Honestly, I never thought I would be here at this stage in my life."

"Hmm. That's something we have in common."

Her eyes widened in surprise. "Really? Do tell."

"I'm not exactly where I thought I'd be at my age

either. I guess you could call me the perpetual bachelor. My friends make bets on how fast I'm going to screw up on a date. While everyone around me is getting married, I'm alone and just burying myself in my work. I'm not exactly what you would call a people person."

"You could have fooled me. I think we're having a very nice conversation."

He nodded. "We are. But you're different from other women."

She wrinkled her nose at him. "Oh, that doesn't sound good."

"No, trust me, it is. Otherwise, I'm sure you would have run out of here as fast as you could after spending five minutes with me." He smiled at her in what he hoped was a friendly grin.

She returned his gesture. "I doubt that. Now let's order some food before all this alcohol goes to our heads and we do something crazy."

"Crazy? That sounds intriguing. What crazy things have you done in your life, Ivy?"

She laughed. "Let's just order lunch, or is it dinner? Besides, I'm definitely not drunk enough yet to tell you all my secrets."

"Fair enough. Maybe over dessert I'll make you spill your guts."

"Maybe," she said and picked up her menu. "So what do you think is good to eat in here?"

****

Ivy had a fantastic meal with Lucas. They ordered chicken wings and nachos—all foods she loved but didn't often eat. They lingered over a shared dessert of red velvet cake and brandy. She didn't want this night to end since she was having such a great time with

Lucas.

Hours before, after the turbulent flight had finally landed, she had made her way through the airport and checked into the hotel. She'd even tried to take a nap in her room, but her mind was spinning from all the tension of the day. Instead of chasing sleep, she had come down to the bar in search of a nice glass of wine. When she saw Lucas sitting there all alone, her heart took a nosedive into her stomach. He was so handsome, and far less intimidating dressed in street clothes, so she had approached him.

At first, he didn't notice her. He had a faraway look in his eye, which indicated he was thinking about some other time or place. That look was all too familiar. She'd seen it many times when she looked in the mirror. However instead of her usual pattern of retreating, she'd worked up the courage to approach him and was glad she had.

After the initial awkwardness of their earlier conversation, they laughed like old friends and shared stories from their past. He regaled her with his tales of quirky passengers on the countless flights he had piloted. It turned out he was based in New York City as well, although he frequently zigzagged the country working. His parents had retired to Florida years ago, and as their only child, he tried to visit them as often as he could.

Ivy told him about her work and her late husband, Matt. He had been more than sympathetic when she had mentioned Matt's brain cancer diagnosis over a year ago and subsequent death from the disease six months earlier. She was close to her parents as well and her sister, Jade. Ivy felt she could open up to Lucas like she hadn't with anyone else. Was it because he was a friendly stranger whom she would likely never see again? No, it was more than that.

His soothing voice and handsome good looks started a fire in her belly she hadn't felt for quite some time. Or was it the two glasses of wine she had indulged in? She couldn't be positive, but she wanted to get to know him better. However, she couldn't be sure she would be able to take that chance—again.

Finally, after they had talked for hours, it was so late, she could no longer keep her eyes open. Although it was only ten o'clock, she had been up since three the previous morning, getting ready for her trip. She had to call it a night, or Lucas would end up carrying her to her room. Not a bad idea. His strong, powerful arms could more than handle her weight. And she imagined, for a minute, how she might feel, safely tucked in his embrace. She shook her head to clear it, hoping her lustful thoughts weren't written all over her face.

"Well," she said, pushing away the last of the dessert. She was so full, she had probably gained five pounds at dinner. "I think I'd better get going. I have to check on my flight for the morning and get some sleep."

"Sure, it is getting late," he agreed and signaled for the check. "Just let me pay the bill, and then I'll walk you to your room."

A few minutes later, they were making their way out of the bar. Lucas didn't say anything, but instead of it being awkward, a comfortable silence settled between them. They both had rooms in the hotel on different floors. Lucas said he would drop her off on six and then make her way up to eight.

He grasped her hand in his as they walked through the lobby. It was large and warm, and she didn't pull away. He caressed her palm with his thumb. She was enjoying this skin-to-skin contact. It seemed like an eternity since she had been touched that way.

Somehow this situation between her and Lucas just felt right, despite her earlier misgivings. But she knew in her heart it would never work between them. She was too damaged from her past to ever be able to love again, and he was such a gentleman. He deserved better than her.

They had arrived at the elevator without her even realizing it. There was an empty car open and waiting. They stepped inside, and the doors closed in front of them. Lucas pressed the buttons for their floors and then he turned to her.

He had a look in his eyes she couldn't quite read. "Okay," he said. "If I don't do this right now, I'm going to lose my nerve…"

His voice trailed off, and before she could reply, he swept her up in the most passionate kiss she had ever experienced. He pushed her gently against the back of the elevator car and pressed his body into hers. She could feel his hard, rigid muscles beneath his clothes, and she melted into him. His hands cupped the back of her neck, deepening the kiss. Then he ran his fingers gently through her hair.

Their tongues found each other and explored with fervor. She tasted the brandy they had shared, it was intoxicating. Reaching out, she touched his chiseled jaw. It was still smooth from a recent shave, and he groaned at the contact. She fisted her hands in his hair.

"Oh, Ivy," he breathed as their bodies pressed

closer together.

She could feel his sculpted muscles tense—all of them. And then the elevator let out a loud ding and announced they had arrived at the sixth floor. It startled them both, and they sprang apart.

"This is my floor," she said ruefully.

"Yeah," he said with a sigh and led her out of the elevator.

Her room was just a few doors down the hallway on the left-hand side. When they reached their destination, she paused with her key in her hand and looked up at him. His gorgeous green eyes were searching hers for some sort of reaction. She smiled to let him know she was okay and let out a long breath.

"Well," she said, breaking the silence. "Thank you for dinner." *And the amazing kiss.* "I had a great time."

"Me, too. Ivy, I want to see you again." He paused as if unsure what to say next.

She was lost in the sound of his deep, sexy voice. The way he said her name was so smooth and inviting. She didn't know what to say to him. Did she want to see him again? Her body screamed yes while her rational mind yelled no.

"Lucas, I don't know," Ivy replied, the war inside her head still raging on. "Look, I really like you. You're a great guy."

"Oh, I've heard this one before. It's the whole, it's not you, it's me thing, isn't it? I know you've been going through some difficult times these past few months, but if you would just give us a chance—no, give yourself a chance—I promise you won't be disappointed. We have a connection. I don't think, no, I know I've never had a six-hour dinner with a woman, ever. And still, after all this time we just spent together, I can't get enough of you. I want to know more, much more."

He leaned down and pressed his lips gently to hers. It was a softer kiss this time, with less urgency, but no less passion than the first. His lips were so incredibly soft, and he wrapped his arms around her, right there in the hallway. Although there were a few other guests milling around, she felt like they were the only two people in the world.

She felt cocooned and safe in his embrace. It was something she had not felt in a very long time and hadn't realized how much she craved it until now. She couldn't bring herself to pull away, even as her mind was telling her she was making a mistake. Ivy leaned farther into him, and her whole body relaxed. Then, whether it was from lack of sleep, too much wine, or too much of a sexy stranger, her vision blurred, went black, and then she fainted.

Chapter Two

Lucas grabbed Ivy around the waist just in time before she hit the floor. She had passed out, and he began to panic. This was a night of firsts that just didn't end. He had never met a woman so enchanting and beautiful. Then he had also never enjoyed talking to a woman over drinks and dinner as much as he had with Ivy. And the kiss—it was a first on so many levels. But it didn't stop there. He had never kissed a woman who then promptly fainted on him. His pilot training kicked into gear before he could lose his mind, and he discovered that her heartbeat was normal, and she was breathing. She'd had a very difficult day; perhaps it had been too much for her.

He would get her inside her room and then call for a doctor. Retrieving her key card from the floor where she had dropped it, he slid it into the slot and disengaged the lock. There were a few soft lights illuminating the room, and he maneuvered her over to the king-size bed and set her down gently on the white duvet.

The room was decorated in soothing tones the color of soft sand, but Lucas, so focused on Ivy, barely noticed his surroundings. He sat down beside her on the bed and watched her for a few moments to see if she would regain consciousness. From his training, he remembered that sometimes fainting spells only lasted a few minutes. He hoped that was the case today. Her light-blonde hair was fanned out on the pillow, and her delicate features stood out beneath her ivory skin.

But underneath that gorgeous exterior was a woman in deep pain—one who had been so rocked by the trials of life and he feared may never love again. His heart had ached for her when she told him about the loss of her husband. She had opened up, but he got the sense she wasn't telling him the whole story. It was a tragic event no one should ever have to endure. That much he understood.

And he got the feeling she was resistant to the idea of getting involved with another man for so many reasons. She didn't want to betray her late husband's memory, that was true. But it was more than that. At the heart of the matter was the fact she couldn't bear to risk loving again with all its possible perils—like another broken heart. Well, he had no intention of letting her down. And furthermore, he made himself a promise not to give up on this beautiful creature. She was one worth fighting for.

The emotional and physical connection they had to each other was electrifying to him. He had seen and felt it throughout their time together tonight. And when he finally took that huge risk of kissing her in the elevator, she had responded to him on a primal level. It was like they were made for each other. Despite this fact, maybe he shouldn't have kissed her; it was too soon. But truth be told, he had been unable to stop himself.

He tore his gaze away from her and moved to call the front desk. They would more than likely know a doctor in the area. But just as he reached for the receiver, Ivy moaned and began to stir.

Lucas dropped the phone and turned his attention back to her. "Hey," he whispered. "Are you okay? You gave me quite a scare."

"Yeah," she replied and opened her eyes. "I'm fine." She tried to sit up but was unsteady.

"Just lie down and rest for a minute." He guided her back down on the pillow and she nodded.

"I'm going to call a doctor just to make sure you really are fine."

She held up a hand. "No, Lucas, please don't. I'm sure I'm okay. I think my blood pressure just dropped. I'm supposed to take medication for that, but I forgot today because I was so busy."

"Where is it? I'll get it for you."

"Over there," she said, pointing to the bag on the dresser. "In my suitcase."

Lucas walked over and rooted through her things. Underneath all the lacy bras and satin underwear— which made his lust for her spike again—he found the prescription bottle. He reached for it and imagined peeling those silky garments from her smooth, pale skin. God, what this woman could do to him, and he'd only known her for less than a day. *Pull yourself together, man. Focus on Ivy and her medicine, not her undergarments.* Grabbing the bottle, he made his way back to her.

He set the pills down on the bedside table and went to fetch her a glass of water from the bathroom. When he came back with the cool glass of liquid, he sat down and eyed her.

"Y'know," he said. "If you wanted to invite me into your room, all you had to do was ask. But there you go, being the big celebrity and fainting in my arms."

"Stop it," she admonished but laughed at the same time. "Thank you for not letting me fall on my face."

"Well, it's a beautiful face, so I couldn't let you damage it."

She paused, and he thought he saw her blush under her ivory complexion. "Now take your medicine, or I'm calling the doctor."

"Yes sir, Captain." She sat up and swallowed a small pink pill with the water he had handed her. Then she looked up at him.

"Well," he said and stood. "I should probably go and let you get some rest, that is, if you're sure you are perfectly fine."

"I am. Thank you again, for everything."

"It was my pleasure," he said and gazed down at her. "Listen, I know you're not sure about all this, but just in case you want to see me again, here's my contact info." He handed her a business card emblazoned with the airline logo and his name, email, and phone number. "My cell number is on the back; you can call me anytime."

She glanced at the card and then set it down on the nightstand. He turned to leave.

"Lucas, wait." She got up and moved toward him. He ached to reach out and fold her into his arms, but he had to resist the overwhelming urge as he didn't want to frighten her away.

They both had a hell of a day, and she had been through a lot. He knew exactly what he wanted—her. But she had an enormous amount of information to process. Time and sleep were the only things that would help her, so that's what he would give her.

Ivy paused a foot away from him and took a deep breath. "I…" Her voice trailed off. "I'm just not sure about anything right now."

"That's okay. Take all the time you need." And with that, he turned and made his way toward the door. He didn't look back for fear his new resolve to give her some space would shatter into a million pieces if he laid his eyes on her exquisite face again. They needed some distance between them for now and then she would come back to him. He could only hope he was right. Lucas couldn't help but think his whole future was riding on this.

****

Ivy stared at the door as it closed behind Lucas. He was gone. She was alone—again. Her heart had screamed out to stop him, but her rational mind took over this time and she stayed silent. She let him go but had she made a terrible mistake?

Ivy had experienced the most fantastic evening with Lucas. The food, the conversation, and the kiss had her feeling like she was trapped in a fairy tale. Not to mention his handsome good looks and easygoing nature. She bared her soul to him about her past, and his words had been tender and caring. The night had been magical for both of them, but it was one which could never have a happy ending. It just wasn't meant to be.

She glanced at his card on the table. She picked it up and turned it over. He had written his number in bold script and had included a personal message to her. It read, *I'm not giving up on us.* She sighed. Well, even if he wasn't, she had to. She wasn't prepared to go through what she had experienced in the past six months ever again. Her heart and soul would not

27

survive a second round.

She changed into her pajamas, brushed her hair and teeth, and then crawled back into bed and switched out the light on the nightstand. Laying her head on the pillow, she spoke to the empty room. "I'm sorry, Lucas Freeman, but I'm not the woman for you."

She was exhausted and soon fell into an uneasy sleep. The same uneasy sleep she'd had every night since her life had fallen apart.

****

The next few days flew by in a flurry of activity. Ivy had made her connection to Las Vegas just in time for the afternoon session of the conference. Then she spent the rest of the week presenting her new speech on the power of perseverance to various information technology experts. It was both exhilarating and tiring at the same time.

She had forgotten how much work these events were, and she was horribly out of practice. But she was back in the game, as her agent would say, and she felt good about it. Most of the people she met were very professional and didn't ask about her personal life. That suited her just fine.

After spilling her guts to Lucas at the beginning of the week, she felt drained. It had been good to talk and get it out, even if she hadn't told Lucas the whole story. But she just wasn't ready to express all her feelings—or move on, for that matter.

Ivy had left Lucas's business card in the hotel room in Denver. After much internal debate with herself, she decided not to contact him. Although he was handsome, charming, and a wonderful listener, she just wasn't ready for a relationship. And she knew he wanted more than friendship from her after that passionate kiss in the elevator. It had flooded her system with lust and desire. Those were two emotions she couldn't quite deal with, and she didn't know if she would ever be able to face them again.

She had just completed her last speech and made her way back up to the hotel room. The conference was being held in one of the most glamorous resorts—The Victorian in Las Vegas. She had been here many times and always loved the hotel and energy of the great city.

The Victorian was dazzling with huge chandeliers and mirrors on every wall. The polished marble floors gleamed. She had wandered through the casino and shops in her spare time. After the conference, she had also eaten at the restaurants in the evenings when she was free. The entire place was elegance at its finest.

Ivy stepped off the elevator on the twenty-second floor and made her way down the hall toward her hotel room. She wasn't leaving to go back to New York till tomorrow morning, so she figured she'd go for a swim in the luxurious pool and order room service. The farewell dinner for the conference was tonight and she had been invited to attend, but she wasn't up to it, so she had declined.

Ivy approached her room and made a mental note to call her sister once she had taken a few minutes to relax. Ivy and Jade were as close as sisters could be. Jade was worried about her, seeing as how this was Ivy's first big trip in over a year. She'd been there for her throughout the whole ordeal of the past eighteen months and was the only one who knew the complete story. Not even her parents—whom she loved dearly but could not confide in—nor Matt's family knew what exactly had gone on after his diagnosis. Only Jade, so thank goodness for big sisters.

When she opened the door, she surveyed the neat and tidy room. The maid must have come in while she was at the conference. The curtains were open, and the bright afternoon sunshine was streaming in.

The room was done up in a lush, rose-colored tone with the furnishings reminiscent of the era the hotel was famous for. The room boasted a king-size canopy bed and a small sitting area with an elegant ivory sofa with claw feet and gold accents. The glass coffee table matched the decor. The only sign of the modern world was the large television mounted on the wall. Ivy found the look full of old world charm, and she loved it.

Setting down her purse, she kicked off her heels and sat down on the sofa. Ivy longed for her yoga pants and a comfortable sweater. She was just about to go and change when the room's telephone sprang to life with a loud ring. It was probably Jade calling. Ivy chided herself for not contacting her sister earlier, but she had been exhausted after her speeches and hadn't been up to talking. Getting up, she made her way over to the ringing phone beside the bed.

She was surprised by the voice on the other end of the phone.

"Ivy, hello," said a smooth, sexy voice she recognized in an instant.

It was Lucas. He was contacting her. Her heart fluttered at the sound of his voice, and she sat down on the bed to catch her breath. She thought she had left him behind in Denver, but here he was, reaching out to her again.

She flashed back to those sensuous kisses they had

shared only a few nights earlier, and her passion for him rose. It was no use trying to stamp it down. He had gotten under her skin, and she let the memory wash over her. The warmth and feel of his touch were soothing and comforting to her battered soul. She wanted to feel that again. But could she let herself do that? She didn't know. But thankfully, she found her own voice. "Lucas, how are you?"

"I'm good. Really good. I just have a layover in Las Vegas, and I thought I would see if you were still here."

"Yes, I am. The conference is all finished."

"How did it go?"

"Very well, thank you. How have your flights been?"

"Better than the one you took with me on Sunday," he said and laughed.

His deep, throaty voice reminded her of his gorgeous smile and luscious lips. Her stomach did a little flip-flop. Goodness. He wasn't even in the room, and he was having an incredible effect on her.

"Hey," he said and broke her out of her wayward thoughts. "If you're not busy tonight, would you like to go somewhere with me?"

Ivy was stunned. Did she want to see this gorgeous, albeit no longer technically a stranger, again? Her rational mind told her to just end it now. It wasn't fair to lead him on when she wasn't ready to date. However, her heart longed to see him again. Could they just be friends? Well, there was only one way to find out. "Umm, what did you have in mind?"

"It's a surprise, but we'd have to leave soon. Are you up for it?"

"That depends on what it is and what I have to wear. I've been in heels and suits all week, and I've had enough of that for a while."

"Ah, c'mon, let me keep you guessing, for now. And it's totally casual, so you can wear anything you want."

Ivy thought for a minute. *What do I have to lose?* Besides, a swim and room service alone hardly held any appeal now given her present offer to spend the evening with Lucas. But she told herself she would be upfront and honest with him about her status. Assuming she could figure out for herself what that actually was.

"Okay, sure," she answered and smiled. "I think it sounds like fun."

"It is, I promise you. Now, can you meet me in the lobby of your hotel in, say, twenty minutes?"

"Sounds good; I'll see you then."

Ivy hung up the phone and let out a long sigh. What was she doing? She had no idea, but the only thing she knew for sure was that after talking to Lucas, she felt more alive than she had since she had lost Matt over a year ago. And she decided to just go with that feeling—at least for tonight.

****

Lucas fidgeted as he waited for Ivy on a burgundy-striped sofa in the lobby of the Victorian Hotel. It was crowded, but he barely noticed anyone as he was too lost in his thoughts about Ivy. He was disappointed she hadn't called him since they'd parted ways in Denver a few days ago. But he also wasn't too surprised, either.

She was a woman still grieving for her late husband, and since he couldn't keep his hands and lips off her on the very night they met, he had scared her away. But she had responded to his advances with the hunger of a woman who needed the attention of a caring man but wouldn't let herself accept it. They had a connection; he just had to prove it to her. Lucas reminded himself he needed to take it at her pace from now on. Otherwise, he may lose her forever, and he was not willing to entertain that idea.

He had experienced a pretty busy week flying back and forth across the country, but Ivy was never far from his mind. Which was a completely foreign concept to him. Usually, after his mostly disastrous first dates, he never thought about the women again. Ivy was unique in that way and so many others.

He had originally wanted to track her down in New York after she got back from the conference, but when he discovered he would be spending tonight in Vegas, he took a chance she would still be here. Since she hadn't contacted him at all, it was his move. After a few quick phone calls, he set up what he hoped would be a very romantic evening.

Now all that was left was for her to show up. Lucas was dressed casually in khaki cargo pants and a well-worn, black t-shirt. He had wanted to look as casual as possible to keep the mood light. Not to mention, it had been unseasonably warm in Vegas, so he didn't need a coat. It was a perfect day for what he had planned.

Just then, he saw her step off the elevator at the far end of the lobby. She was a vision with her long hair loose and wavy and her violet-blue eyes. She turned more than a few heads as she walked by, and Lucas found himself feeling possessive of her. He didn't want anyone leering at her like a few of the likely drunk hotel guests were. *Take it easy. She's not yours—yet.*

He stood up and walked over to meet her. Ivy hadn't spotted him, so he took this opportunity to study her. She looked fresh-faced and was dressed in jeans and a blue sweater which brought out the beautiful color of her eyes. Her easy grace was obvious from the way she walked. She hid her pain well in public, but he knew it was still there. Finally, she noticed him, smiled, and walked over. Her smile was genuine with beautiful, straight white teeth, but it didn't quite reach her eyes.

"Hello again," she said as she approached him.

"Hi," he said and tried to keep his voice steady. God, he wanted this woman more than he had ever wanted anything.

Lucas was caught off guard as she reached out her arms to embrace him. He recovered in an instant and enveloped her slim frame. This felt so right. He inhaled the fragrance of her perfume. She smelled of sweet roses; it was an intoxicating scent. When she kissed his cheek and stepped back, and he took her hands in his. The feel of her delicate lips on his face sent his desire for her skyrocketing.

"So," she said and smiled. "Where are you taking me on this beautiful day?"

"You'll see when we get there." She let go of his hands and put hers on her hips in a mock gesture of annoyance.

"Okay. But I have to be back by midnight, or I'll turn into a pumpkin."

He smiled down at her. At six-foot-two, he was a lot taller. "I doubt that," he said and laughed. "But we'll be back before then, I promise. Let's go. The car is waiting."

Leading her out of the lobby, he guided her

through the large glass automatic doors of the front entrance. The dry desert air hit him all at once. It was a bit of a shock from the cool, air-conditioned hotel. The busy driveway was bustling with people, cars, and luggage, but Lucas only had eyes for Ivy.

He led her over to a shiny, silver vintage car that had been lovingly restored. Opening the door, he gestured for her to step into the vehicle.

"Wow," she gushed, sitting down in the passenger seat. "This car is fantastic. Where did you get it?"

Lucas slid into the driver's seat and smiled at her. He was relieved she liked the car and didn't think it was an old relic like some of his previous dates had. "I rented it from a classic car place in the area, but I've got my own back in New York. I have to admit, I have a thing for vintage cars." *And you.*

"That's great," she said. "My mom and dad are actually into classic cars, so I grew up around them. I don't have a car, but if I did, it would have to be one like this."

"Well, I'll be sure to take you for a spin in mine when we get back to New York."

"Sounds great."

They fell into a comfortable silence as Lucas started the car. The engine roared to life, and he weaved his way onto The Strip. The traffic was heavy, but they soon turned onto the highway, and the glitz and glamor faded into the background. They were making their way out of the city, and desert landscape soon replaced fancy hotels. Lucas put on the radio, and they listened to classic rock music and enjoyed the scenery around them.

After about half an hour, they turned off the

highway and headed into Boulder City. When they arrived at the municipal airport, Ivy let out a squeak that Lucas thought was adorable. *Well, at least she's surprised.*

"Lucas. What are we doing at an airport?"

"Trust me, okay? Just give it a chance."

"I'm not so sure," she said and bit her fingernail.

Lucas pulled into a parking spot and took her small hand in his large one, preventing her from chewing off her nail.

"It's a helicopter ride," he said. "They are completely different from those commercial planes that freak you out. Since you said you didn't like flying, I was pretty sure you'd never seen the Grand Canyon from the sky."

She looked at him with wide eyes. "No, I haven't. And there is an excellent reason why."

"Believe me, you won't regret it. The scenery is so extraordinary, you'll forget you're even flying. And this experienced pilot will take care of everything."

"What?" she exclaimed. "You're flying the helicopter?"

"Of course. I'm the best there is, if I do say so myself. Besides, I don't want to share you with anyone. I want to be the only one to see your reaction to one of the wonders of the world from the best view around."

"Okay," she replied, unconvinced. "But be forewarned. My reaction might involve an airsickness bag."

He smiled at her. "You'll be fine, I promise. Now, do you want to go and get a coffee while I do the final checks on the helicopter? And just so you know, we will be flying a single engine helicopter. It has one main rotor with an anti-torque tail configuration. It is one of the safest in its class."

"I'll take your word for it, Captain, since none of that except the safe part made any sense to me."

"Good. I won't explain any further, lest I bore you to death. I should just be a few minutes. Go inside and make yourself comfortable. I'll come and get you when we are ready to fly."

Ivy smiled and turned to make her way inside the terminal. Lucas watched her go with desire for her burning deep inside him. She was perfect in every way. He wanted to give her the night of her dreams. Well, it was time to make that happen. He turned toward the tarmac feeling happier than he had in a very long time.

Chapter Three

Ivy made her way into the airport terminal and found the café easily. It was a small area, so she couldn't get lost. The place had large windows that looked out onto the tarmac and was painted the color of a cloudless sky. She went ahead and ordered two decaf coffees. The girl at the counter was cheerful as she handed Ivy her order.

Ivy had decided to forego the caffeine; she was already jittery enough from seeing Lucas again. Not to mention the thought of the helicopter ride. That alone was making her nerves jangle. She should have known a pilot would want to take her on a flying date. But could she handle it? *Relax. It's just another plane ride.* Besides, Lucas was right. A helicopter wasn't the same as the commercial planes she normally flew in.

"Keep telling yourself that," she said aloud as she sat down at one of the vacant tables to wait for him.

Back at the hotel lobby when she first laid eyes on Lucas again, her heart fluttered, and she felt a yearning rise up in her. She found herself drawn to his warm embrace, and she had this hard-wired instinct to feel his arms around her. And when she reached for him, he didn't back away. Instead, his strong arms encircled her, and she felt safe and protected. That was not a feeling she had become accustomed to in the last year, but she now knew she craved it like desert plants craved water. While it probably wasn't a good idea to get used to him, she just couldn't help herself in that moment.

She chided herself for leading him on. After all, she had promised herself she would be upfront and honest with him. And not only did she openly embrace him, she kissed him on the cheek. His soft, just-shaved skin warmed her lips, and she inhaled his masculine scent mixed with white musk cologne. But friends hugged and kissed each other all the time, right? Yeah, but they didn't have the feelings she was having right now.

Feelings of lust and desire welled up in her, and she found herself wondering what it would feel like to have his muscular arms hold her tight, all night long. *Stop it right now. You can only be friends with him, nothing more.*

Just as her heart was getting ready to fire back a response to her rational brain, in walked Lucas with a huge grin on his face. Good thing she was sitting down because her knees went weak. With his intense green eyes and golden-streaked hair and goatee, he looked like a sexy surfer, not a pilot. Well, he probably did that, too. He seemed to only have eyes for her, and she didn't quite understand why. There was so much wrong with her right now, but he didn't notice or care.

"Hey," he said as he took the seat across from her at the table. She handed him the coffee, and he took a sip. "Thanks. The helicopter is ready for us. Are you all set?"

"I guess so." She took a large gulp from her cup and finished the last of her coffee.

Lucas reached across the table and took her hand. His touch was soothing and reassuring to her. She felt a calm wash over her when they were connected. But still, it wasn't meant to be.

Then she made a decision to just let herself enjoy it, if only for tonight. They were far away from New York City and all the ghosts that lurked there. She would be back to reality soon enough, and her bruised heart desperately needed a break from the stress and strain of life. It would all be waiting for her when she got home tomorrow—alone. But right now, there was a handsome, kind, and gentle man who wanted to be with her. She was going to make the most of it.

"Trust me, okay?" Lucas said and gazed deep into her eyes.

And this time she gazed right back at him. "I do," she said and meant it.

He rose from the table still holding her hand. Then he led her over to the departure area and smiled at the man behind the desk. The man looked like he was in his mid-sixties. He had a deeply lined, tanned complexion but wore a friendly expression.

"Hi, Paul," Lucas said to the man.

"Hey, Lucas. All ready to fly? And who is your beautiful companion on this wonderful afternoon flight?"

"This is Ivy. Ivy, this is Paul." Ivy shook hands with the man and returned his smile. "Paul has been running this place for as long as I can remember. He's the best."

The man laughed. "Well, Lucas is one of my favorite customers and an excellent pilot. But I have to say, you are lucky, Miss Ivy, because Lucas usually flies solo. You must be one special lady for him to ask you to soar with him."

Ivy felt her face flush to what she imagined was a deep crimson, but she still managed to smile back at Paul.

"She is," Lucas replied and moved toward the door. "Bye, Paul. See you around eight when we land back here."

"I'll be here. Have a safe flight."

"Will do," Lucas called over his shoulder as he put an arm around Ivy. They stepped through the double doors and out onto the tarmac. The air was still dry and hot as Lucas led her over to the waiting helicopter. He opened the door for her and she hopped up. After shutting the door tight, he made his way around to the pilot's side and got in beside her.

Lucas handed Ivy a pair of headphones and helped her buckle up. Then he flipped a bunch of switches, and the machine sprang to life. Once they were ready for takeoff, he radioed to the control tower. Lucas confirmed their departure, then reached over and gave Ivy's hand a squeeze. She gave him the thumbs up sign, and the craft rose up into the air.

Ivy watched as the craft flew higher and higher in the sky. The view really was spectacular, and they were still at the airport! They headed west, and the landscape grew more and more magnificent as they flew. Houses and buildings gave way to vast desert scenery. The sky was clear blue with a few wispy clouds hanging about. The small desert trees and bushes looked like toys from this height.

Ivy was so excited about all of the breathtaking sights, she forgot all about her fear of flying and relationships, at least for the moment. She was having a wonderful time as Lucas showed her all the points of interest that they encountered as they flew. They saw the magnificent Hoover Dam, which he told her held the largest body of water in the Southwest. Then they passed Eagle Point, which was the home of the famous Skywalk Glass Bridge. The people were tiny pinpoints from their vantage point, and the bridge was glimmering in the late afternoon sun.

The Grand Canyon itself was extraordinary. Ivy could hardly believe she had never wanted to see it before. Lucas was right—she was truly missing out on a great wonder of the world. Ivy was surprised to hear from Paul that Lucas often flew alone. With his handsome good looks, she hadn't believed him when he said he rarely dated. Maybe it was true.

They had reached the West Canyon by now, and Lucas said he was going to set the helicopter down so they could look around. Ivy was pleased. She was having a great time, and it just kept getting better and better.

A few minutes later, he set the craft down and killed the engine. Lucas turned to Ivy and removed her headphones.

"Are you having a good time?" he asked and she could sense a touch of nervousness in his smooth, deep voice.

"The best," she replied and launched herself at him.

He took her in his arms and laughed his low, sexy laugh.

"I'm glad. Now, do you want to go for a walk or eat first? I brought a picnic basket with stuff I hope you like."

"Let's walk around first and then eat." It was so

sweet of Lucas to bring them a meal. He had thought of everything.

"Sounds perfect," he said as he reached for her seat belt to unbuckle her. His hands brushed across her breasts and abdomen, and she felt a shiver of desire run through her. She flushed but was relieved when he didn't notice. He got up, exited the helicopter, and ran around to her side to open the door for her. He grasped her hand to help her as she stepped out into the interior of the canyon.

She looked up and marveled at the view. The rock formations were magnificent. Shades of orange and red boulders sculpted by winds, rain, and time from the Colorado River shot up into the sky. Ivy was lost in the beauty of this exquisite site. She forgot all sense of time and space and just stared at the spectacle. Lucas was quiet beside her, and then she noticed he was gazing at her in all her wonderment.

"You were right," she breathed out. "This view is amazing."

"Well, I'm not going to tell you I told you so, but…"

"You did, I know," she said and laughed.

He grabbed her hand again and led her to the rugged gravel path just a few feet away from the helicopter. "We can take this path for quite a while and then turn around and come back. There are a couple of caves along the way. But let me know whenever you are tired, and we can head back. I know you've already had a busy week."

"No, I'm ready to see it all. Let's go." Ivy felt a surge of excitement rise up in her. She knew it had to do with the spectacular view, but it also had to do with

Lucas. Her earlier weariness was long forgotten.

They walked for a couple of miles and then found a quiet vista to sit down and enjoy the view. Lucas spread out a blanket and placed a cooler down on top of it. The sun was beginning to set, and Ivy was struck once again by the beauty of the landscape.

After they sat down on the blanket, Lucas opened the cooler and took out a bottle of champagne. He popped the cork and poured her a glass. Then he opened a can of cola for himself.

"What's all this?" Ivy asked with a glimmer in her eye. She was touched by everything he had done for her.

"A toast," he replied. "To you. Your successful conference and your first trip to the Grand Canyon. And it's all yours. Only soda for the pilot. I need to get you home in one piece."

"Oh, Lucas, you shouldn't have."

"I wanted to. You deserve it. You've been working so hard."

"Thank you," she said, accepting the glass from him. He held up his can and the tin clinked with the glass. He smiled at her again. "To Ivy and her successful week. And to her first of many trips to the Grand Canyon."

She smiled back at him. "And also to you, Lucas," she added. "For bringing me to this magical place. It means so much."

Tears welled up in Ivy's eyes, and Lucas moved closer and put his arm around her. She could smell the white musk scent of his cologne, and despite herself, she leaned into him. "Hey," he said as he handed her a tissue. "What's the matter?"

"It's nothing," she replied and looked away from him. She was so overwhelmed by all of his kindness and caring, yet she couldn't be with him. It was just too much. Her emotions were getting the best of her, and she didn't know what to do about it.

It was time to be honest with Lucas, but she really didn't want to ruin the mood. She looked back at him and saw concern etched on his handsome face. His emerald-green eyes were searching hers. She had to say something, but what? Taking a deep breath, she found her voice.

"It's just that you went to so much trouble for me. It's so thoughtful of you. I'm not used to that."

"You should be, Ivy. This and so much more. You deserve to be happy, and I want you to have a wonderful future ahead of you—one that I hope includes me."

"Lucas, it's just that…well…it's complicated."

"Try me. You can't keep carrying this burden by yourself. It's going to wear you down—or worse. Trust me. You can tell me anything."

"I know," she said and drew in a shaky breath. She gulped the last of her champagne in one swallow. The alcohol was hitting her hard as she hadn't had anything to eat since lunch. But without that liquid courage, she doubted she would have been able to tell Lucas anything.

"Okay," she said. "Here's the truth. You are a smart, charming, and handsome man, and I'm hopelessly attracted to you. But we just can't start dating like some normal couple."

He looked at her with a confused expression. "I feel the same way about you. So why not?"

"Because I'm damaged goods."

He frowned. "No. You're not."

"Lucas, you barely know me."

"But I want to."

She shook her head. "Well, you might change your mind if you knew…"

"Give me a chance," he said as he touched a warm hand to her cheek.

"I don't know if I can."

"Why?"

"Because of Matt. I loved him, but he changed after he was diagnosed with brain cancer. Then he died and left me alone. I can't go through that again; I won't survive. Besides, I feel like I'm betraying his memory if I even think about another man the way I can't stop thinking about you."

"Ivy, c'mon. Do you really think Matt would want you to live the rest of your life alone? If he was a good man—and from what you told me he was—he wouldn't want this life of seclusion you have chosen for yourself. He would want you to live and love again."

She closed her eyes and continued to speak. She'd come this far, she might as well tell the whole story. "It's more than that. I lost Matt a long time before he died. In fact, after his diagnosis, I don't have any happy memories of us."

"What do you mean?"

"I've never told anyone this," she replied. Then she took a deep breath and began to explain. "You see, when Matt was diagnosed with brain cancer, he withdrew from me. And because of the nature and fast progression of his illness, things went from bad to worse. I wanted to support him, but the more I tried, the more he pushed me away. And when he got worse, he'd hurl insults and yell and scream at me for hours on end. Sometimes he would hit me, but he was often too weak, thank goodness. It was the disease that made him that way—and of course, I knew that—but it was hard to take."

Ivy stifled a sob. Lucas took her hand with a tender touch and nodded for her to continue. "In the end, he didn't even know me, and although that, in itself, was devastating, it was better than the rage he had directed at me earlier. I hid all the abuse from his parents and mine. I didn't want his memory tainted with all the horrible things he had said and done when he wasn't in his right mind. The only person who ever knew was my sister, Jade. I can't hide anything from her. So you see, Lucas, I'm not the girl for you. I'm too messed up."

"That's not true, Ivy. You had the courage to face whatever cards life dealt you, and through it all, you were kind to everyone. Those are not the qualities of a broken woman, but rather, one who is strong beyond belief. I'm not giving up on you—on us. You deserve another chance; we both do."

Ivy was openly sobbing now, and Lucas just held her tighter. She didn't, couldn't push him away. He was opening her up in a way she believed she never would again. She wasn't going to make any decisions tonight, but maybe she should consider the possibility of a future with Lucas. She sniffled, blew her nose, and then looked up at him.

"I'm a mess," she said and laughed at herself. "You should probably run back to the helicopter and take off before you get any more involved with me."

"Nonsense. You look beautiful. Sad, but beautiful.

And I'm not going anywhere. I'll stay right by your side as long as you'll have me." He smiled down at her. "We'll get through all of this—together. And we'll take it at your pace from now on."

"Okay," she said and tried to smile back at him. "I'm sorry, Lucas. I've ruined the mood."

"No, you haven't. You have to open up, Ivy. I'm just glad you chose me. Now let's have some dinner and more champagne." He refilled her glass and got out some fruit, cheese, and bread from the cooler.

They shared a comfortable silence as they ate. Lucas stayed close to her, enveloping her in his warmth, and she felt safe and comforted in his embrace. From this vantage point, they watched the brilliant orange sun slip slowly below the horizon. The sky turned from blue to a deep violet, and the temperature was dropping. But tucked in Lucas's powerful arms, she barely noticed the chilly night air.

They walked back to the helicopter after they ate, and Lucas pointed out a few of the sights in the semi-darkness. Ivy took his hand for the walk. She wanted to feel connected to him, and this felt safe enough. He never let her hand go until they arrived back at the helicopter, and he helped her inside for the ride back.

The trip back in the helicopter and the car ride from the airport went way too fast for Ivy. She had wanted this night to last forever. Tomorrow it was back to reality and all its problems.

When they arrived back at the hotel, Lucas walked her up to her room. He was staying at a hotel down the strip from her, but he insisted on making sure she made it safely back. When they reached her door, she turned to him. "Would you like to come in for a drink?"

"Umm, are you sure you're up for it?"

She smiled. "Yes, I'm positive. And I have a fully stocked mini bar that has been neglected all week."

"Okay. One drink for me, and then you need to get some rest. You have a long flight home tomorrow."

She smiled up at him and opened her door. "You, too," she chided. "And you actually have to fly the plane."

He laughed. "Don't worry about me; I'm used to it." They stepped inside. "Wow, this is a great room," he said as he looked around. "I've never stayed here."

"Yes, I love this hotel. I come here a lot."

Ivy went over to the fridge and took out a bottle of wine for herself. Then she turned to Lucas. "What would you like?"

"Is there any whiskey?"

She produced a small bottle and held it up for his approval. "Perfect. I'll go get some ice."

A few minutes later, they were seated on the comfortable sofa with their drinks, chatting like old friends again. Ivy was enjoying Lucas's company, but she was starting to feel sleepy. She stifled a yawn.

"I should get going," he said, rising to stand. "You're tired, and it's been a long week for you."

Ivy stood up and grabbed Lucas's hands in hers. She looked up into his big, gorgeous green eyes and saw an intense affection for her. Ivy wasn't ready to be intimate with him, but she didn't want him to leave, either. "Lucas," she said. Then, almost in a whisper, she asked him a question that came straight from her heart. "Would you stay with me tonight and just hold me?"

"Of course," he said, pulling her into his arms. She inhaled his white musk scent, and her whole body relaxed.

"Go on and get ready for bed. I'll be here."

Ivy smiled at him and then made her way into the bathroom.

****

When she had shut the door behind her, Lucas let out a long exhale. He was making progress with Ivy, that was for sure. Their heartfelt conversation at the canyon had helped him see her pain and hesitation firsthand. He was shocked to learn she was suffering not only from the loss of a husband but also from all that went on with his illness. It was staggering to think she was already back to work.

Now it was his job to help her work through the relationship side of her life. She had bared all her secrets to him, and he didn't take that lightly. It took a lot for her to open up, but he was glad she had. She needed to talk about it, and he was grateful that he was able to be there for her.

But he wasn't sure how he was going to pull all this off without losing his mind. His attraction to her was unlike any other he had experienced. He wanted her body and soul, naked beneath him. But that wasn't going to happen for a long time—if ever.

He poured himself another stiff drink and turned out all but the nightstand light. The room was warm and dark now, and he kicked off his shoes and socks. He then shrugged out of his t-shirt and took off his pants. Now bare-chested and only wearing his boxer briefs, he went over to the bed and turned down the fluffy comforter and sheets.

He downed his drink and climbed into bed. The sheets were cool in contrast to his flaming skin. He was on fire for Ivy. Laying his head down on the pillow, he took some deep breaths and tried to relax.

He had managed to gain control of himself by the time Ivy emerged from the bathroom. But as soon as he saw her, he almost lost it again. Her face was freshly washed and devoid of makeup, but she looked more beautiful than ever. Her hair was brushed and shining. She was dressed in pink pajama shorts with a matching tank top. Lucas's eyes had adjusted to the dim light, and he took in the smooth, bare flesh of Ivy's arms and legs. He wanted to caress every part of her and peel off those thin layers of clothing that did nothing to hide her trim figure.

Easy, he reminded himself as she made her way toward him. She seemed hesitant now, and Lucas wondered if she had changed her mind about him staying. He sat up in bed and tried to hide his unbridled lust for her. "Do you want me to go? It's okay if you changed your mind." It might be better for both of them if he left. She was almost too tempting in her present state, and his self-control was hanging on by a thread.

She sat down on the other side of the bed but didn't look him in the eye. The room plunged into darkness when she switched off the nightstand light. He could hear the sound of her breathing, but she didn't say anything for a few long moments. Lucas threw back the covers and started to get up. He would just go. She wasn't ready for any of this—for him—and he wasn't going to push her.

Suddenly, she grabbed his arm. Her touch was cool and light. "No, please stay," she said and pulled him toward her as she lay down. Her back was to him as she got under the covers. He put an arm around her, and she curled into him.

They were flesh to flesh as his bare chest cradled her small frame. Lucas leaned over and stroked her beautiful, long hair that was flowing freely down her back. He planted soft kisses on the back of her neck. Then he lay his head on the pillow behind hers. He inhaled her fragrant scent of fresh roses. She began to whimper, and Lucas's head shot up in alarm. He could see her tear-streaked face in the darkness and, with a gentle touch of his fingers, he wiped them away. She was coming undone, and he couldn't help but think this was all his fault. "Ivy," he whispered, his voice full of concern.

"I'll be okay," she said so low and soft he almost didn't hear her. "Just keep holding on."

And so he did.

Chapter Four

Ivy awoke from a dreamless sleep late the next morning. She felt warm and heavy, and when she tried to move, a strong arm tightened around her. Lucas. He had held her all night, and she'd experienced the best sleep she'd had in over a year. She felt rested—really rested. As she carefully wriggled out of his soothing embrace, he rolled over onto his back but didn't wake.

She opened her eyes and gazed at him. His handsome face was relaxed in sleep, and his golden-streaked hair was pushed back from his forehead. She reached out and touched the soft strands. His tanned, muscular, bare chest stood out in contrast to the white sheets, and she now noticed he had several tattoos on his upper arms. Tribal bands snaked his right arm, while his left was an intricate design of the sun and moon together. She laid her head on his warm torso and lightly traced the beautiful art with her fingers.

Lucas let out a sigh and opened his exquisite green eyes. "Morning, gorgeous," he murmured in his smooth, deep voice. "Sleep well?"

"Yes, the best. Thank you, Lucas, for everything."

"You don't have to thank me, Ivy. I wanted to be here. And I'm glad you got a good rest," he said and pulled her into his arms again. She allowed herself to be swept up into his comforting embrace, and the feeling of his rigid muscles tightening around her made intense desire well up in her. She should feel guilty for sharing her bed with another man. But somehow she didn't. *Maybe there's hope for me after all.*

After a few minutes, she lifted her head off his chest and looked up at him. "I wish we could just spend the day in bed but—"

"That sounds good to me."

She smiled at him and suddenly realized he had made her smile again, which was something else she hadn't done in longer than she could remember. "I have to get up, or I'll miss my flight."

"I can get you a later flight," he offered.

"No, I really need to get back to New York." For what, she had no idea. She had nothing and no one to look forward to, but she needed to process everything that had happened in the past few days. And she couldn't do that with Lucas, in all his half-naked glory, lying beside her. He was much too distracting and tempting. She didn't want to do something they might both regret later, and with the current wayward thoughts running through her mind, that was a distinct possibility.

"Okay, sure," he said, almost as if he could read her mind. He kissed her on the forehead and moved to get out of the bed. She watched as his lean, muscular frame stood. When he stretched his powerful arms and legs, she was almost overcome with passion for him. Oh boy; she wanted him.

He gave her a questioning look but didn't say anything. Goodness, was she that obvious? Well, she was horribly out of practice with this kind of stuff, so it would be best to move on and pretend they were just friends, right? *Whatever. You have no idea what you are doing.*

"I'm going to grab a quick shower. Is that all right?" Lucas asked. His voice pulled her back into the present moment.

"Sure, go ahead. I'll pack up my things, and I'll get dressed when you are done."

Lucas sauntered into the bathroom, and the sound of the rainfall shower echoed out into the bedroom. He hadn't shut the door, and she silently wondered if that was an open invitation for her to join him. Ivy flashed to an image of him. She had already seen him half-naked in her bed, and her imagination filled in the rest. The water would cascade down his sculpted muscles, and his hair would darken when wet. She contemplated how it would feel to run soapy hands all over his naked body. Then the shower suddenly let out a screeching sound as Lucas turned it off, and Ivy was startled out of her daydream.

She was flushed, and she shook her head to clear her thoughts. After all the crying and carrying on she had done with Lucas over the past few days, she thought maybe he was just being polite by staying with her. And perhaps once they parted ways today, he might try to get as far away from her as he could.

He poked his head around the corner and startled her again.

"You okay?" he asked, as he stood a few feet away from her, wearing only a towel around his slim waist. Water droplets glistened on his bare chest, and his hair was indeed darker and slicked back from his face. He looked like a Greek god with his muscular torso and arms.

Ivy sighed and looked away. She'd better get

herself under control. She didn't want to lead Lucas on, as she wasn't sure what was going on with her.

Lucas seemed to pick up on her uneasiness and came over to stand with her by her suitcase. He grabbed her hands in his and led her over to the bed to sit down. Not knowing what to do, she sat too, but couldn't look him in the eye.

"Hey," he said and lifted her chin with a finger so she was forced to look at him. "You don't need to be embarrassed about last night. I completely understand. I'm just glad I could be there for you."

Ivy felt a blush creep up her cheeks. Was she embarrassed about last night? Yes, she had never opened up to anyone. Even her sister hadn't seen this side of her, but it was more than that. She was also incredibly attracted to this half-naked man sitting beside her, and this intense attraction was something she could no longer ignore. From the kind words Lucas had just spoken to her, it didn't look like he was going to bolt as she had theorized earlier.

Ivy willed herself to be strong. She owed that not only to Lucas but also to herself. Gazing up into his beautiful eyes, she saw they were full of immense concern for her. The slight frown and worried expression she saw on his gorgeous face made her feel even more guilty. She had put that look on his face, and she wanted to erase it. Could she do it? She wouldn't let him leave like this—all worried and concerned about her—and she wanted to show him she could handle this.

His eyes were searching hers, waiting for a response. Instead of answering him, she climbed onto his lap and gazed at him. He seemed surprised, but his muscular arms encircled her, and she reached up to put her hands around his neck. She lifted her chin and pulled his lips down to meet hers.

"Ivy," he breathed. "It's okay if you're not ready."

Ivy could feel his heartbeat quicken in response to her touch. She smiled. "Just kiss me, Lucas."

She had barely gotten the words out when his mouth crushed hers in a wave of passion. Their tongues found each other and they intertwined. She tasted mint toothpaste and could smell the fresh scent of the hotel soap on his damp skin. He cradled her head in his hands and ran his fingers smoothly through her hair.

They sat together, locked in this moment for a long time. Ivy felt cared for, cherished, and safe in his arms—feelings she thought were lost to her.

Lucas pulled away first and pressed his forehead to hers. "God, you're so beautiful, Ivy," he whispered. "Where have you been all this time?"

"Lost," she replied. "But you've finally found me."

They kissed again at a slower and deeper pace. Time seemed to stand still for them. They were two lost souls who had come together at last. Lucas ran his powerful hands down her back and pressed her closer to him. Ivy put her head on his sculpted chest and listened to the comforting sound of his beating heart.

He pulled away and spoke to her in his low, sexy voice. "I'm going to need another cold shower."

She smiled with a sad expression. She wished she could give him more—all of her—but she just wasn't ready. "Lucas, I—"

"Shh," he responded and wrapped her further into his embrace. "This is perfect. I promised to take it at your pace, and I meant every word. This is more than I had hoped for, and we'll get there. It's just going to take some time. But now that I've got you, I'm never letting go."

Ivy sighed and leaned into him. She just hoped he was right, that one day she would be ready for more.

****

Half an hour later, Lucas was driving back down the Strip to his hotel room to pick up his things. They had shared another passionate kiss before he regretfully left her to get ready for her flight. It tore him apart to leave her side, but he if he hadn't, there would be regrets for both of them. She had turned him on like no other woman had before, and it took a second ice-cold shower in her hotel room before he was under control again.

Lucas reached his hotel in record time. He had been so distracted by thoughts of Ivy, he could hardly remember how he got there. That wasn't good. Lucas called his co-pilot, Ben, to make sure everything was on schedule for their late afternoon flight back to New York.

"Hey partner," Ben said. "What happened to you last night? I thought we might hit the casino and grab some dinner, but you were incommunicado."

"Yeah, sorry about that, Ben. I went to see...a friend."

"A lady friend? Perhaps the beautiful Ivy?"

"Perhaps," Lucas replied and tried to keep his tone neutral.

"Oh, c'mon. Don't hold out on me. Did you see her or not? How did it go? Has she finally come around to the charming ways of my best friend?"

"Okay, okay. Too many questions at once. Yes, I

saw her. It went well. I hope to see her again, and that's all you are getting out of me."

"Well, we'll see about that. We've got a marathon flight across the country later today, and I'll bet you'll get so bored, you'll tell me every last detail."

"Maybe," Lucas said. "But hey, speaking of the flight, is everything on track?"

"We're all set. I called in to confirm our take-off time half an hour ago. So I'll see you at the airport, say four o'clock?"

"Sounds good. And Ben, thanks for asking about Ivy. She's becoming someone special to me."

"Well, I'm glad to hear it. You've been alone too long, and if Karen sets you up with any more of the girls she knows, you will unfriend me for sure."

"Not a chance, buddy," Lucas said and laughed. Ben's wife, Karen, had been unsuccessfully setting him up with all her single girlfriends the entire year. Lucas was getting tired of it, but he went along with it because he knew she meant well. However, he couldn't help but breathe a sigh of relief those days were over.

"Well, I'll see you later on then," Lucas confirmed.

"For sure," Ben said, and they both hung up.

Lucas wanted to do a quick workout in the hotel gym this morning and then try to get a few hours of rest. He had spent half the night watching Ivy sleep, and while he hadn't regretted a moment, it was catching up with him. Nevertheless, he couldn't go to work in his current state of mind. His thoughts were racing with images of Ivy's sensuous body. A good run and round of weights would help burn off his extra energy and improve his focus. And then he could crash for a few hours before he had to be in the air.

After this flight, Lucas would have a few days off, and he had to get some things in order. His condo looked like it had been ransacked by burglars, and he hadn't done laundry in quite some time. He was also going to see Ivy again, and he was encouraged by the way they had left things. His plan was to show her some of the wonderful sights in New York City, and there were a few intimate restaurants he wanted to take her to. She was coming around slowly and he understood. He had to fight with himself to go at her pace, but he was determined not to mess things up like he had in the past.

Once in particular, a year or so back, he'd fallen hard for a girl, and he had pushed her too fast. Looking back, it was more lust than love, but it hadn't seemed like that at the time. She was a free spirit and hadn't been ready for a serious relationship. One day, Deanna had packed the few things she left at his place when he had been out of town on a flight, and left him a good-bye note. He had never seen or heard from her again.

After that, he became the serial dater he had told Ivy about. He had second- guessed his every move and rarely had a second date with anyone. Lucas had been given a chance with Ivy—a fresh start—and he wasn't going to fail this time. He owed it to both of them. Reinforcing his silent promise to himself, he grabbed some sneakers and headed to the gym.

****

When Ivy arrived back in New York City, she was startled by all the sights and sounds of Christmas which had enveloped the city in her absence. There was snow on the ground, and all of the shops boasted Christmas decorations and festive items for sale. This would be

Ivy's first Christmas without Matt.

But last Christmas, he was almost lost to her anyway, and it hadn't gone well. In an effort to keep his escalating abusive behavior a secret, she had told family and friends he was ill and the two of them were going to stay home and keep things quiet this year.

But to try and get his spirits up, as well as hers, Ivy had bought Matt many nice presents and cooked a fancy turkey dinner for the two of them. Matt had become furious with her over dinner, telling her he hated the presents, then he hurled his entire plate full of turkey, potatoes, and vegetables across the table at her. Ivy had fled to the spare room. She locked the door and cried herself to sleep. He had died seven months after that fateful day.

This year, Ivy would be alone, and all her friends and relatives would look upon her with that pitying stare she loathed. Everyone she knew was married or at least dating, and she would be the only single one at all the gatherings. But there was Lucas. He was so great—charming, caring, and devastatingly handsome. Despite this, she wasn't ready to tell her family about him yet.

They wouldn't understand. Everyone assumed she should still be grieving for Matt and she was, in her own way. But it was almost two years now since she had been happily married, and since then she had been through a lot. She needed to move on, and no one would understand why she was rushing things. In fact, she knew Matt's family would be horrified she was even thinking about another man. He had been their only child, and they doted on him his entire life.

She wanted to keep Lucas to herself—for now. And she did well with that promise until one day the following week when she was having lunch with Jade. Ivy had been avoiding her sister, and Jade insisted they meet at their favorite bakery for lunch and catch up. Ivy, feeling guilty, had agreed.

She had been out with Lucas the previous evening, and he had taken her to an intimate French restaurant Ivy had heard of but hadn't been to. They had shared a wonderful candlelight dinner. It was very romantic. Afterward, he had walked her home and kissed her senseless outside her apartment door. Ivy was still beaming from the memory, and she was seeing him again later today. She couldn't hide her excitement from her shrewd sister's gaze.

"You look...different," Jade commented as they placed their orders for soup and fresh baguettes. "What's going on with you?"

"Nothing. Just glad to be back working, you know." Ivy tried to lie, but she wasn't good at it. Especially when it came to Jade.

"That's good. But it's more than that, little sister. Tell me what's happening."

Jade had a no-nonsense tone she took in all her dealings as a New York City detective and, unfortunately, with Ivy, who was only three years her junior. But it always made Ivy feel like a little kid who instantly confessed what she was trying to hide, and it worked again today.

"Well...it's just I met someone on my trip to Vegas."

"Met someone?" Jade asked and raised her eyebrows. Clearly, she hadn't been expecting that. "Who? Where? When?" She rapidly fired the questions at her baby sister, just as she always did.

Ivy paused. She didn't want to say too much, but if she didn't say enough, her sister would keep prying until she got answers. Best to just stick with the facts, and the fewer, the better.

"Umm, a pilot. The one who flew the plane. He recognized my name on the passenger manifest and introduced himself. I met up with him again when we had the layover in Denver. Then he called me after the conference, and we ended up going for a helicopter ride in Vegas."

"What?" Jade exclaimed. "Why am I just hearing about this now?"

Because I didn't want to tell you. But just like always, I can't hide anything from you. That wouldn't go over well. Ivy tried another tactic. "Well, we've both been busy and haven't had a chance to properly catch up. Besides, I'm not sure it's really going to turn into anything." Ivy tried to sound casual but failed miserably.

"Hmm," Jade replied. "I think there is more to this story than you are telling me, so spit it out. Is this pilot the reason you are practically glowing? I can see it, you know. You can't hide anything from me."

Great. So much for keeping Lucas under wraps. She sighed and tried to explain. "I know. It's just I'm not really sure of anything myself. I met him; he's a great guy. He's handsome, funny, and kind. We've gone out a few times, but it's not serious yet. Besides, I don't think he's ready for me and all my excess baggage."

"Ivy Castlefield," Jade said and joined hands with her sister over the table. "You deserve to be happy. And if this fancy pilot is the one to do it, don't let him get away. Who cares what anyone else says or thinks? You and I know the truth. It's been too long since you've so much as looked at another man."

Ivy smiled at her sister. Jade always knew what to say to her, and she didn't pull any punches—just the hard, cold truth. Despite her misgivings, it was refreshing to finally tell someone about Lucas. "Thanks, big sister," Ivy said. "I'm glad you dragged the story out of me."

Just then their food arrived, and the two women enjoyed a few minutes of silence savoring their soup. The bakery had the best butternut squash soup Ivy had ever tasted. The warm broth had a hint of sweetness Ivy had not been able to duplicate at home. Just as she began to relax, her sister started up again.

"So," Jade said, "does this handsome pilot have a name?"

Ivy sighed and tried to figure out how to survive the next round of questions.

****

A couple of hours later, Ivy and Lucas took a stroll through Central Park. It was snowing, but it wasn't bitterly cold. They were both dressed for the weather in warm parkas and heavy boots. Lucas had suggested the walk to her yesterday at dinner.

He loved to walk when he wasn't flying since his occupation itself could be very confining. And he was back at it tomorrow, so he wanted to stretch his legs as much as possible before his long work week began. He was going to suggest they pick one of the many street vendors to get something to eat later, and he hoped Ivy would like that. They strolled arm in arm through the late afternoon crowd, most of whom seemed in a big hurry to get somewhere. But Lucas and Ivy were content to just walk and take in the sights.

"How was lunch with your sister?" Lucas asked as they passed an elderly couple holding hands.

Ivy groaned and rolled her eyes. "Not good. Don't ask."

"That bad?"

"Worse than you can imagine. I love her, but she's always grilling me for information—and getting it. She's probably running a criminal background check on you as we speak. I'm surprised she didn't get your social security number out of me. But thank goodness I don't know it, and don't tell me!" Ivy laughed and pulled Lucas in closer to her.

"Oh, she's just looking out for her baby sister. And being a detective, I'm sure she sees too much in her line of work."

Ivy nodded. "I know. You're right. It's just I wasn't quite ready to talk about you. But unfortunately for me, it was written all over my face."

Lucas smiled and leaned his face down toward Ivy's. "And what a beautiful face it is." Then he kissed her right in the middle of Central Park. It was like when he was with her, no other place, time, or person mattered—except her. He just hoped she was beginning to feel the same.

He pulled her closer to him and inhaled her rose scent. She tasted even sweeter, like the cherry candy canes he had bought for her today. Ivy said they were her favorite candy, and she had been indulging in them throughout their walk.

After a few desire-filled moments, he pulled away. He was getting carried away with her in the middle of a crowded park. A few people clapped and cheered, and Ivy turned as bright red as her scarf. But Lucas didn't care. He wanted everyone to know she was his. He turned to her, hoping she wasn't too upset and tried to switch gears.

"Want to grab something to eat?"

Ivy smiled up at him. Her cheeks returned to their natural color. "Sure. I saw a hot dog vendor back over the hill. I don't usually eat those, but well, when I'm with you, I am finding I'm not my old, boring self, so let's go for it."

"You could never be boring to me," Lucas said and smiled at her. "Just look at this crowd you've attracted by taking advantage of me in public."

"Oh please." Ivy laughed. "Don't start. I've already had a difficult day with my sister at lunch."

"I know. Let's go eat."

A few minutes later, they were seated on a bench by one of the many ponds in the park. They both held jumbo hot dogs loaded with all the fixings. Beside them were two steaming cups of hot chocolate. Lucas was suddenly having second thoughts about the casualness of this date.

"Hey, are you okay with this?" he asked. "Y'know, we can go to a restaurant and eat, if you'd rather."

"Don't be silly," she replied and smiled at him. "This is perfect. I'm having a fantastic time."

Lucas returned her smile. He spotted a dab of mustard at the corner of her mouth and kissed it away. She laughed. "I'm a mess, aren't I?"

"Not even close." He put his free arm around her.

They sat in a now familiar silence for a few minutes, enjoying their meal and people watching.

Adults and children alike were out, playing or walking in the light snowfall today.

"Hey," Lucas said, breaking the silence. "What are you doing for Christmas?"

"Ugh," Ivy groaned. "You had to go and ruin the mood, didn't you? I have family gathering after family gathering lined up, and all my relatives will look at me with their pitiful stares. I have half a mind to just stay home and avoid the whole thing. How about you?"

"Oh, I'm sorry. Well, I have some vacation to take because I was too busy working this year to take it earlier. So I'm off for a week."

Ivy smiled up at him. "That's nice. Are you going to see your family in Florida?"

"Well, I was thinking about that, and then I had a better idea."

"Oh yeah. What's that?"

"I was thinking of taking my gorgeous new girlfriend to see my favorite state for a week. She desperately needs a break from her family this year. I've already booked a couple of hotel rooms and two flights. Now all I need is for her to agree to go."

Ivy's eyes widened in surprise. "Lucas, are you serious? Where do you want to take me?"

He smiled. "Very. And how does Christmas in Hawaii sound?"

Ivy looked stunned, and Lucas wondered if he had gone too far booking everything for a romantic week on the beach in Oahu. Of course, it could all be canceled at a moment's notice, and from the look of uncertainty in Ivy's eyes, he was just about to suggest that. Instead, without warning, Ivy threw her arms around his neck and kissed him hard on the mouth.

"Yes," she exclaimed. "When can we leave?"

Chapter Five

Exactly two weeks later, they were lying on the delicate sand of Waikiki Beach and soaking in the soothing rays of the sun. It was heavenly. Ivy felt like she had been spirited away to paradise, and the sight beside her was very pleasing to the eye.

Lucas was bare-chested and wearing dark-gray board shorts. His sculpted arms and torso stood out under his naturally tanned skin, and his hair, damp from their recent swim in the ocean, was slicked back from his face. Dark shades hid his gorgeous eyes. But he was watching her.

And he was getting quite a few looks from people passing by—all women, of course. But he only had eyes for her. She was dressed in a cute little black bikini she had picked up in a specialty shop in New York. It hugged her curves in all the right places and showed off her figure well. They were a striking pair. But as far as Ivy was concerned, they might as well have been on a deserted island. This week was all about them, and neither Lucas nor Ivy had any intentions of letting anyone inside their inner circle.

Ivy stretched out on the luxurious beach blanket they were sharing. Lucas leaned over and kissed her on the cheek.

"Are you having a good time?" he asked, leaning in close to her ear.

"The best," she said and took his face in her hands. She loved his rugged look with his goatee and five o'clock shadow. They kissed deeply with much passion, and Lucas pulled her into his powerful embrace. When they came up for air, he whispered to her, "Sure beats eggnog with the relatives, eh?"

"Yes," Ivy said. "Whosever idea this was, it was a great one."

"I take full credit."

Ivy laughed and pushed him away playfully, but she didn't get far. He held her tight. His comforting arms were soothing to her battered soul, and she felt like she was beginning to heal—one step at a time.

Her family had indeed been surprised when she told them she would not be joining them for Christmas. Only Jade knew the whole truth, and she was completely supportive of Ivy's choice. She promised she would cover for her and try to smooth things over with their disappointed parents.

Jade had told her she needed to start doing things for herself. This was something she had been neglecting in recent months. Although she had said yes to Lucas, she had immediately started having second thoughts. Jade set her straight and helped her pack her bags last night. Then she told her to have a wonderful time and send her some pictures of the beach. It had been snowing non-stop in New York, and Ivy was more than excited to get away from it all.

They met at the airport, took an overnight flight, and arrived on the island that morning. Since they had both slept on the plane, Ivy wanted to hit the beach right away. It was a gorgeous day, and they had spent it walking in the surf, swimming in the ocean, and lounging on the soft sand.

It was now late afternoon, and the sun was beginning to dip low in the sky. Lucas leaned over to her. "Do you want to go and get ready for dinner? We have reservations at the Luau Restaurant in the hotel."

"Oh, Lucas, you are spoiling me."

He nodded. "Yes, and I want you to let me, if only for this week."

"Okay," Ivy replied. She was having a fantastic time with Lucas, but he had refused to let her pay for anything. Ivy was an independent woman, so she kept insisting—and he kept refusing. But she didn't want to make an issue of it and ruin the mood, so in the end, she had acquiesced.

"I guess I'd better go get cleaned up. I'm pretty sure bikinis aren't on the dress code at the restaurant."

Lucas looked her up and down with a hot stare. "Well, it's okay with me, but…"

"C'mon, let's go," Ivy said laughing, as she rose and shook the sand off her legs. "Just promise we can come back here tomorrow. It's so beautiful and tranquil, very un-New York, which is exactly what I need."

Lucas chuckled at her. "I'm glad. Now let's get going. I'm starving."

She grabbed his hand, and they walked the short distance to the hotel. It was one of the nicest on the beach, and Ivy had marveled at it earlier. Lucas had booked them into two side-by-side rooms with an exquisite view of the ocean. He walked her to her suite and then went to his room to change for dinner. They agreed to meet in the hotel bar in an hour.

Ivy looked around her spacious room. It was

tastefully decorated in tones of soft gold, and it was warm and inviting. There was a large fireplace along the wall. When they had arrived this morning, she had just dropped her stuff and they headed for the beach. Now she took in the scene before her. It was really sweet of Lucas to get her a room of her own. But did she need it? She still wasn't sure. The king-size bed looked plush and comfortable, but was it too large for just one person?

Ivy decided to take a luxurious bath in the spa tub. It would help her clear her mind. She went into the bathroom and turned on the tap. With the water flowing, she added some rose-scented bubbles. She stripped off her bikini and climbed in. The temperature was perfect, and she leaned back and inhaled the flowery scent of the water.

Lucas wasn't pushing her to be intimate. After all, it was he who had gotten them separate rooms. But she had never felt this close to a man before. Sure, she had loved Matt, but that was different. They were high school sweethearts who grew up together. This relationship with Lucas was more—adult. Still, she was horribly out of practice in the bedroom. But it was like riding a bike or something like that, wasn't it?

She sank down in the water and tried to enjoy this tranquil time. *Just go to dinner and then see what happens.* Maybe she would surprise herself. Lucas made her feel different, but she wasn't making any decisions right now. The bath was warm and inviting, and it slowly pulled her into a state of utter relaxation.

****

Lucas sat at the bar an hour later, dressed in a black suit with a violet tie, waiting for Ivy. He looked around the space, and a woman who sat alone at the far end of the bar tried to catch his eye. But he purposely ignored her stare. The only woman who mattered to him was Ivy. He ordered a beer for himself and a glass of white wine for her as he settled in to wait.

He was glad she had agreed to come away with him this Christmas. It had been a tough decision for her since she was close with her family, but he wanted—no needed—to get to know her better. His family had been disappointed they weren't joining him as well, but since he frequently crisscrossed the country for work, he had missed more than a few family gatherings. Ben was spending the week with Karen's family, but he made Lucas promise the four of them would get together as soon as they got back.

Lucas took in his surroundings. The bar was an open concept, set in the middle of the lobby. Quite a few people were milling about as it was now happy hour. Everyone looked relaxed. He didn't suppose you could be any other way in this island paradise. This trip and the setting here couldn't have been more perfect for them. Hawaii was Lucas's favorite destination, and he wanted to share it all with Ivy.

They'd had a wonderful day at the beach, and this was just the beginning. Ivy was becoming more affectionate with him, but he wasn't expecting anything more from her. She had been through so much and needed time to heal. But for his own sanity, he had gotten them separate rooms. He didn't think his willpower could withstand a week of bikinis and lingerie. And of that, he was sure after he had admired her beautifully proportioned body all day at the beach. She was slim but had curves in all the right places. An image of her flashed in his mind that kindled a blaze of desire. Lucas was thankful they were meeting fully clothed for dinner. His libido needed a break.

But as he saw her walking toward him from the bar entrance, he realized he wasn't going to get one. She had exchanged her little black bikini for a little black dress, and the form-fitting lace number left little to the imagination. It had tiny straps which showed off her toned shoulders and ended mid-thigh. Her ivory legs were bare and high- heeled sandals completed the look. Waves of white-blonde curls floated around her.

Lucas was astounded. She was even more beautiful than he thought possible. He recovered his composure and waved her over. She smiled as she saw him and sauntered his way. "Control yourself, Freeman," he said aloud. "She's not ready for your unbridled lust."

"Hi, gorgeous." He could feel the tug of an easy grin as she approached him. Ivy had made him smile more in the past month than he had in years. "I got you a glass of wine."

"Hi, handsome." She leaned into him. He took her in his arms and inhaled her sweet rose scent, which made his desire for her surge. They kissed, and it brought him close to the edge. He was in for a week of ice-cold showers at this rate. Their lips parted, and she smiled and took a seat beside him at the bar.

"Thank you," she said, accepting the goblet from his outstretched hand.

"Well, I hope you like it. They have five kinds of white wine, and I had no idea what you would prefer."

She took a sip. "It's perfect. I love it. Thank you, Lucas, and not just for the drink—for everything."

"Ivy," Lucas said, taking her hands in his. "You

deserve all this and much more."

"Oh," she said as her eyes filled with tears. But he knew they were tears of joy this time. "Stop it, or you'll ruin my makeup."

He hadn't noticed she was wearing any. She was a natural beauty. "Okay," he said, and he kissed her forehead. "But just so you know, it's true." They finished their drinks holding hands and enjoying each other's company.

****

After that, they walked over to the garden themed restaurant, and Ivy marveled at the beauty of this five-star hotel. It had all the comforts of home and none of the problems. It was paradise at its finest. The restaurant was located outside and was enclosed in lush, tropical setting, just as the name promised. The sky was just beginning to darken into a pretty lavender, but the air was still warm.

The perky, young hostess led them to a secluded table surrounded by palm trees and hibiscus plants. Ivy could hear the soft sound of rushing water and noticed some large fountains adorning the space.

After being seated, she explained the evening's specials to them. The hostess ensured them a waiter would be with them shortly. Ivy was having a fantastic time with Lucas. He looked so dashing and refined in his suit. She was glad she had thought to pack a few dresses; this restaurant was a fancy one.

The waiter arrived, and Ivy ordered a pina colada. The island was famous for its pineapples, and she couldn't wait to taste them. Lucas ordered another beer, and they perused the menu. They had roasted pig, which the restaurant highly recommended. Lucas said he was going to order that. Ivy wasn't feeling quite so adventurous, so she opted for the catch of the day which was served with rice and vegetables.

Their meal arrived, and they ate with gusto. Ivy hadn't noticed how hungry she was until now. The fresh ocean air was like a balm on her frayed nerves, and Lucas was helping her immensely, too. Somehow, tonight all her problems seemed far away, and that's where she wanted them to stay.

Ivy ate her entire meal and was still hungry. Lucas suggested she order dessert. She asked for a slice of coconut cream pie, and they both ordered coffee.

"Lucas," Ivy said as she took a bite of the pie. Then she got instantly sidetracked. "Oh my goodness, you have to taste this."

Before he could protest, she scooped up another forkful of pie and fed it to him.

"Mmmm," he murmured. "It's good."

Ivy took another bite and savored the rich, creamy flavor of the dessert. The crust was soft and flaky, and it melted in her mouth. She closed her eyes and tasted the fresh coconut flavor. When she opened them again, Lucas was smirking at her.

"Sorry," she gushed. "I don't usually eat dessert."

"No, go right ahead," he said. "I'm enjoying watching you."

She rolled her eyes at him. "Oh stop. You're embarrassing me."

"Okay," he said and sipped his coffee. "But you were pretty cute."

She just smiled back at him.

Darkness had fallen by the time they had finished dinner, and Ivy asked if they could go for a walk on the beach. "Of course," Lucas said and led her to an access gate at the back of the restaurant.

The wind was blowing softly, and they stripped off their shoes. When her feet touched the sand, Ivy noticed it was cooler now. She shivered and Lucas offered her his jacket. After shrugging it on, she took his arm.

They walked quietly for a few minutes. All of the hotels were lit up for the night in grand splendor. Ivy spent a few minutes looking at the beautiful sights. Although she had been to Hawaii—several times, she had spent little, if any, time on the beach as she had always been working. This trip was different in the best way possible.

They walked partway down the beach and a cool breeze rose up from the ocean. Ivy let out another shiver, and Lucas pulled her in close to him.

"Let's head back to the hotel; you're cold," he said.

"Okay." She was having such a wonderful time, she didn't want it to end, but she was beginning to catch a chill. He seemed to notice her hesitation and gazed at her with a tender expression.

"Hey, don't be sad. We have all week in this beautiful paradise."

"You're right," she replied, as she snuggled deeper into his embrace.

When they reached her room, Lucas offered to get the fireplace started. Ivy agreed and said she would order them something to eat and drink from room service.

She was hungry again. At this rate, she thought her bikini might not fit by the end of the week. But she had been neglecting her diet, and her hunger was just another indication she was healing. So she took it as a positive sign and ordered them a plate of exotic cheeses with dessert wine. It was perfect.

She slipped off her high-heeled sandals and made her way over to Lucas, who was leaning over and fiddling with the fireplace.

He smiled up at her. "I think I've got it going. Come here; sit down and get warm."

He motioned to the place beside him on the luxurious Persian rug that was laid out by the fire. She sat down, and he put his arms around her. The swirling red, orange, and yellow flames dancing about were a calming sight, leaving Ivy more relaxed than ever.

The room service arrived a few moments later, and Lucas set the tray down in front of them. They sipped the sweet wine and nibbled on the delicate cheese selection.

Ivy ate and drank her fill, but she still felt a deep hunger inside—one that food could not satisfy. She desperately wanted to be intimate with Lucas, but she was scared. Of what, she wasn't sure. He had been nothing but the perfect gentleman since they met.

And then it dawned on her. She was afraid of falling in love. In love with Lucas. If they slept together, it would push her in that direction. She debated with herself for several long minutes. Lucas was quiet during this time as if lost in his own thoughts. Finally, her rational side won out. Both she and Lucas were grown-ups, and she was ready for an adult commitment—one he had wanted since the day they had met.

Ivy put her wine and cheese aside and leaned into his comforting arms. She could feel his rigid muscles beneath his dress shirt, and a shiver of desire ran through her. Lucas didn't speak, but his breathing was steady, and she savored the moment a bit longer. Then she looked up into his gorgeous green eyes.

He looked down at her with a longing she knew he could no longer hide. Their lips met in a blaze of passion. It ignited the intense craving they both had for each other. She tasted the sweet wine in his kiss and ran her hands through his hair, pulling him closer.

Ivy reached for the buttons on his shirt to undo them. She needed to feel his flesh beneath her hands. They continued to kiss as her nimble fingers worked the buttons free. Lucas shrugged out of his shirt and laid Ivy down carefully on the soft carpet. He hovered over her, and she caressed his rock-hard torso.

"God, Ivy," Lucas breathed, "I want you..." His voice trailed off as he planted kisses along the side of her neck and the top of her breasts.

"Lucas," Ivy replied, "I want you, too."

He pulled her up, and they were almost eye to eye. "Are you sure about this? Because if you're not, we should—no we must stop right now." He shook his head as if to clear his thoughts and started to get up.

She reached for him and put her arms around his neck to stop him. Then she pulled him closer so their faces were only inches apart. "I'm ready, Lucas," she said in a whispery voice, "for us to be...together. I'm on the pill, Lucas, take me...now."

She barely got the words out when he scooped her up in his strong arms and carried her over to the king-size bed. He set her down gently and leaned over to unzip her dress. She slipped it off, and Lucas gave her an admiring look as her body was clothed only in a black lace bra and matching panties.

"Ivy, you're so beautiful."

She offered him a shy smile and reached for the waistband of his suit pants. Her hands were shaking as she caught a hold of his belt buckle.

"Hey," he whispered, putting his hands over hers to steady them. "Ivy, if this is too much—"

"No," she said, cutting him off. "It's just that, well, I'm really rusty when it comes to this stuff."

"Don't worry; me, too." He took her hands and put them on his sculpted chest above his heart. "See how fast my heart is pounding for you?"

She smiled at his intimate gesture. "Yes."

"So let's agree to take it slow. And if you want to stop at any time, just say the word."

"Okay." But she didn't want to stop—ever. Lucas's tender words had made her want him even more.

She lay down on the bed and pulled him on top of her. He kissed her breasts, her flat stomach, and then he moved down to her delicate lace panties. He kissed her there, and she moaned with pleasure. He carefully removed the scrap of fabric and leaned down toward her sex. Planting soft kisses on her, she writhed beneath him. His tongue darted in and out of her soft folds and it began to drive her wild. She called out his name as a shuddering climax overtook her and released all the pent-up tension she had been fighting.

He moved off her, and she grabbed at the zipper of his pants. His rock-hard reaction told her he was ready for her. She wanted to feel him inside her, and he understood her urgency. He swiftly removed his trousers and boxers and then lay beside her in all his naked glory. She climbed on top of him. He unhooked her bra and threw it aside. Then, with a gentle touch, he took her breasts in his large hands and massaged them. She moaned softly and reached out to stroke his manhood. He shivered and let out a sigh. She guided him into her slowly, and they rocked back and forth. He took a hold of her hips and set the tempo. His breath came hard; increasing with every thrust. Soon, he let out a primal cry and came growling her name.

She continued to move him in and out of her, and soon she was experiencing another earth-shattering climax. They had both let themselves go, finally giving into their carnal urges.

Ivy collapsed on top of him. They were both slicked with sweat. She waited a beat until their breathing normalized. He put his strong arms around her and pulled her down on top of him. Lucas was still buried deep inside her, and she relished in the feeling of their connection.

"Ivy," he whispered. "Are you okay?"

"Yes. Everything is perfect, Lucas. No regrets."

He let out a sigh she knew he had been holding. "Good," he said, and he began to move inside her again.

****

Hours later, Lucas was still awake and gazing at Ivy. She was so exquisite and serene in sleep. The moonlight from the open window caught her white-blonde hair fanned out on the pillow, and it sparkled. He could hardly believe they made their way to each other. Hoping she wouldn't awake in the morning with regret, a frown crossed his brow.

Well, they were only moving forward from this moment. He wouldn't let her go, now that he had her. With that thought etched in his mind, he wrapped her in his warm embrace and lay down on the pillow beside her. The soft sound of the ocean waves lulled him to sleep, and he felt more fulfilled than he had in a very long time.

****

The next morning was another beautiful day in paradise. Sunlight came streaming into the room and awoke Lucas at an early hour. Ivy was still fast asleep beside him. Then it dawned on him. It was Christmas Day. They had shared their most intimate gift—each other—on Christmas Eve. He remembered he had bought a small gift for Ivy, and he quietly crept out of her suite to retrieve it.

He grabbed a quick shower in his room and dressed in khaki cargo shorts and a black t-shirt. His mind was already forming a plan for this special day. He had wanted her to have a glorious holiday to try and make up for her last year of heartache. After ordering breakfast from room service, he let himself back into her room.

A longing stronger than he'd ever experienced built as he watched her sleep. She opened her eyes and smiled at him as if sensing his gaze.

"Morning, beautiful." He leaned down to kiss her.

"Mmm," she answered in response as he swept her up into a passion-filled embrace.

When their lips finally parted, she curled up in his arms and gazed up at him. "Oh my. How late did I sleep?"

"Not very. We still have the whole day ahead of us. Merry Christmas, Ivy."

He produced a small box which was wrapped in gold foil with a red ribbon and handed it to her.

Her mouth opened in surprise. "Lucas, you shouldn't have."

"I wanted to. I know how much you love this holiday, and this year I was hoping to make it special for you. You've been through so much this past year. All I want to do is make you happy."

"You already have, Lucas. This trip, last night. Everything is perfect. I don't deserve you."

"Hey," he said and took her hand with a tender touch. "Of course you do. Don't think like that." He leaned down and kissed her forehead. "Go on, open it."

Ivy removed the ribbon and unfolded the paper. He had spent hours picking this out for her and hoped she liked it.

She opened the box carefully and let out a gasp. "Oh, Lucas, it's so pretty."

It was a diamond-accented layered pendant in the shape of a double infinity symbol in sleek white gold. It was stunning. At its center was a single, large diamond.

Lucas let out a long breath. He was so relieved she was pleased and relished the beautiful smile on her face. "Not half as pretty as you are," he whispered.

She threw herself into his arms and clung to him. He kissed her and inhaled the faint smell of roses that lingered on her skin. He ran a hand down her naked body, and she shuddered with pleasure. She tugged off his t-shirt, and he lost himself in the ecstasy of the moment.

Suddenly a knock sounded at the door. Ivy was startled and then moved to cover her naked body. Lucas cursed under his breath. He had forgotten the breakfast order. Thinking he might just ignore it, he reached for Ivy. But the spell had been broken—for now. He groaned. "Relax. It's just room service. I hope you're hungry." He was but only for her. "Let's continue this later..." He let his words hang in the air.

Ivy smiled up at him. "Yes, that's an excellent idea. Now let me run into the bathroom. I'm a wreck."

"You look stunning to me," he said, with desire heavy in his voice. She smiled and jumped up. Then she ran toward the bathroom. He grabbed for her and she laughed, sidestepping him. She closed the door, allowing Lucas a moment to get himself under control. Then he sighed and went to answer the knocking that had started again.

****

Twenty minutes later, they were seated on the large balcony, enjoying the stunning view of the ocean. The table was laid out with coffee and various breakfast items. Lucas had ordered at least half of the menu and Ivy smiled. He had thought of everything.

She sipped her coffee, which was mixed with cream and sugar, and stared across the table at her new lover. He was still bare-chested, and she drank in the sight of him. Ivy had showered and was dressed in black shorts and a purple tank top.

Ivy loved the necklace Lucas had given her, and she put it on immediately. She had got a gift for him as well and presented it to him as he was heaping bacon and eggs on his plate.

"What's this?" he asked as she handed him a rectangular box.

"Well, you don't think I forgot to get you a Christmas gift, do you?"

"Ivy, all I wanted for Christmas was you, and my wish came true."

He pulled her down onto his lap and she laughed. "Me, too. But I thought you'd like this as well."

"Ivy, really…" he protested.

"Just open it, or you can sleep in your own bed tonight, mister."

"Okay, okay," he said and laughed again. "That would be a fate worse than death, so give me the box."

She smiled and handed it over to him.

He tore off the green and red wrapping and opened the box. Inside was a stunning stainless steel watch. It had a black face and silver hands. Ivy had thought of Lucas when she saw it. The style would go nicely with his captain's uniform.

"Wow, Ivy. It's spectacular. I love it. But it's too much."

She pursed her lips at him. "So is a trip to Hawaii, but you made me promise not to fuss, so I expect the same from you."

He nodded, took it out of the box, and put it on. It looked striking on him.

He grinned at her. "Okay, you got me."

"Yes, I do, Lucas Freeman. You're right where I want you."

She closed her eyes and kissed him softly, and he returned the intimate gesture. When they finally came up for air, she spoke. "Okay, I'm starving again. Let's eat."

But her hand remained tucked in Lucas's as she got up and moved to her side of the table. Ivy chose a bowl of oatmeal and fresh berries to eat. She wanted to have a healthy breakfast, and it looked fantastic. But she barely tasted her meal. She couldn't help staring at Lucas from across the table. He looked so carefree and handsome. When he caught her looking at him, he reached across the table for her other hand.

"So," he said to her, ignoring his food and focusing on her. "Feel like a hike today?"

"Yes, that sounds wonderful. Where are we going?"

"To the top of that." Her eyes followed his hand as he pointed into the distance.

"Wow." She took in the sight of the Diamond Head volcano sparkling in the early morning sun. She knew of it but like most of Hawaii, she hadn't experienced it. "I'd love to. Have you been to the peak before?"

"Yes, but never with someone like you."

She laughed. "Always the charmer, eh? I thought now that you've had your way with me, you'd back off."

"Not a chance," he said and leaned over the table and took her face in his hands. "Now that I've had a taste of you, it just leaves me wanting more."

Instead of replying, she kissed him.

He kissed her back and then raked her body with an erotic gaze. "Maybe we should just spend the day in bed…"

"No way; you promised me a hike. Besides, I'm sure the view from the top is magnificent. So finish your breakfast and let's go."

"Okay." He laughed but kept his eyes locked on hers, and she almost lost her resolve. No, she wanted to get out there and see some sights. She'd make it up to him later.

When she told him so, he whispered, "I'll hold you to that."

****

Half an hour later, they were at the base of Diamond Head, preparing for the climb to the top. A taxi had brought them to the site, and Lucas smiled as he watched Ivy taking in the spectacular view.

"It's so high," she said in awe.

"Only seven hundred and sixty-two feet."

"What?"

"Oh, c'mon. It will only take us about an hour to get to the top. The tour looks like it's starting. Let's go join them."

He took her hand in his and led her over to the small crowd huddled around a petite older lady who would be their guide to the top. Although Lucas had heard the history of the place many times before, he listened in so he could talk about it with Ivy later. He watched as Ivy was intently paying attention to the local woman. Lucas smiled and was glad she seemed to be having such a great time.

"This volcano is made from a two-hundred-thousand-year-old rock," the guide said brightly. "It was given its name by the British soldiers who discovered it in the nineteenth century. They mistook the crystals on the adjacent beach for diamonds. Now let's begin our three-quarter-mile hike to the top."

"I love all this history," Ivy gushed.

I think I love you. Wait. What? Lucas shook his head. *Where did that come from?* "I do, too," he said in reply and tried to rein in his wayward thoughts. It was just that seeing her here enjoying herself, he suddenly imagined he could spend the rest of his life like this. With her. Making her happy. *Easy, Freeman. I don't think she's ready for that.*

Lucas finally noticed Ivy was staring at him.

"Everything okay?" she asked with concern in her voice.

He was daydreaming—again. Plastering a smile on his face, he tried to pull himself together. "Sure. Let's head to the top."

They followed the four other people who rounded out their group and began the trip up to the crater's rim. There were lots of staircases, but both Ivy and Lucas were in great shape, so they climbed them without much effort.

They started up the first one, which had seventy-four steps. Lucas was enjoying the view of Ivy as he walked up behind her. Her short shorts showed off her long, toned legs, and her thin tank top left little to the imagination. He wanted to reach out and grab her, then take her to a secluded corner of the mountain, and have his way with her. But he didn't want to ruin her fun with his lustful thoughts, so he kept them to himself.

The next set was ninety-nine steps, and the last one was a beautiful spiral staircase of forty-three steps. They had finally reached the top, and Ivy let out a cry of joy. "We made it," she exclaimed as she threw her arms around Lucas's neck.

He kissed her hard; he couldn't help himself. Ivy didn't seem to mind and returned his affection. A few of the other tourists gaped in awe at them, so he stepped back. He didn't want her to be embarrassed, but she didn't even notice the onlookers.

Instead, she grabbed his hand and ran across the coastal observation platform to the very edge. "It's so gorgeous," she said. He agreed, but the site of her was all he could focus on right now.

She pointed out to the distance. "You can see the

entire Oahu coast from here and far into the Pacific Ocean."

"Mmm," he murmured. He didn't trust himself to say more.

His arms encircled her waist from the back, and she pressed her body into his. It was almost his undoing. He needed to get her back to the hotel, or he thought he might lose his mind. When he kissed her neck, she giggled.

"Hey, aren't you interested in the view?"

"More than you know," he replied.

She laughed and snuggled closer to him, and they stood in a comfortable silence, taking in all the glory this island had to offer.

****

A couple of hours later, they were back in Ivy's suite, naked and dozing in each other's arms. They had made it back down the mountain with Ivy chatting with enthusiasm about what they had just seen. Lucas had tried to pay attention, but his sensuous thoughts had made it difficult.

When they arrived back at the hotel, she seemed to understand his need and led him to her room. Once there, they had made mad, passionate love for a couple of hours straight. Afterward, his hunger for her ebbed— a little bit. He knew she was tired, so he was going to let her sleep for a while.

Lucas needed to check in with work about next week's schedule, so he moved to get up from the bed. Before he stood, he took a moment and gazed at Ivy. He sensed she was becoming comfortable with him and relished the thought. Although they had only been intimate a few times, they were able to read each other's bodies like they had known each other forever. She fulfilled a desperate need in him, while at the same time, driving him to the edge.

She appeared to be fast asleep to him, so he slipped into his room to grab some lounging pants and his laptop. When dressed, he set up his computer on the desk back in her room. He wanted to watch her sleep as he worked.

Twenty minutes later, Ivy moaned in her sleep. He looked up from his work, concerned. She was writhing on the pillow and shaking her head. "No," she screamed. Bolting up from the desk, he ran to her side. He took a hold of her to wake her up, but her nightmare went from bad to worse.

"Stop. Get off me. You're hurting me," she yelled. Her eyes were still closed.

Lucas gently shook her and attempted to awaken her. "Ivy. Wake up. It's just a dream; it's not real."

"Don't do this, please..." Her voice trailed off.

Lucas started to panic as she wasn't responding to him. *What the hell is going on?*

A little more forcefully, he grabbed her and called her name in a loud voice. Her eyes flew open and she gasped. She was breathing hard and looked confused.

"Hey," he soothed as he took her in his arms. She was sobbing.

"Shhh, you're okay.You're here now, with me."

She sat up and looked at him. "Lucas, I'm sorry—"

"There's nothing to be sorry for, Ivy. Do you want to talk about it?"

She looked uncertain for a moment and then spoke. "It's just that, well, I get these nightmares sometimes— disturbing dreams where Matt is hurting me like he used to when he was sick."

"Oh, Ivy," Lucas said, his voice full of distress as he took in the sight of her tear- streaked face and frightened expression. He pulled her close and inhaled her rose-scented skin. *What did her late husband do to her?*

"What can I do?"

She reached for him. "Just hang on to me. It always passes, eventually."

He took her in his arms and rocked her. Her sobs subsided, and he lay her down on the pillow. He covered her with a warm blanket and lay down beside her.

"Go back to sleep. You still look tired."

She shook her head. "No, I can never sleep for a long time after these nightmares. But I have them less and less, especially now that I've met you."

He smiled at that, but nevertheless, he was deeply concerned.

"Have you seen anyone, you know, to deal with it?"

"Yes, I saw a psychologist after Matt died. I told everyone it was for the grief, but the truth was, I wanted to get to the bottom of these disturbing dreams. She helped me work through it—and it's better than it used to be—but I still get them sometimes."

"Ivy, I'm so sorry."

"Don't be. You're helping me more than any doctor ever could. I just hope you don't think I'm some crazy lady now and want to run screaming from the room."

"Not a chance," he said as he enveloped her in a warm embrace. "Now do you want to rest some more?"

"No. Let's go to the beach. The sunshine will chase this all away."

"Sure," he replied, trying to keep his tone light. "Let's go catch some rays." And they did.

****

Ivy had encouraged Lucas to keep his room for the rest of the week since she thought he might want a break from her. Clearly, she had been mistaken. They spent every moment together, asleep and awake. She was mortified he had seen her have a nightmare, but she hadn't had another one since he had begun sharing her bed. He didn't let her sleep alone anymore, and it helped.

He was so caring and understanding when she had opened up to him about her past. Nothing could keep them apart. She felt like she had stepped off the cliff of her former life and into paradise.

They spent most of their time relaxing on the beach, but Lucas wanted to show her the island as well. One day they took a taxi to the Honolulu Farmers Market in town. Ivy had said she loved visiting them in New York, so Lucas suggested they check one out here.

They wandered around for hours, sampling the local cuisine and talking to the artisans. Everyone was friendly and warm. They tried fresh pineapple smoothies and sampled honey and chocolate made right there on the island. For lunch, they dined on fresh mahi-mahi with rice and corn. They shared a dragon fruit shaved ice for dessert, and Ivy was full again—both physically and spiritually.

"I love this place," Ivy gushed after they had finished their big meal. "The entire island is so fascinating."

"I'm glad," Lucas responded, pulling her close and putting his strong arms around her waist. "This is my favorite state in the whole country, but I've never had a vacation as wonderful as this one, Ivy. I love spending time with you. You make me feel alive."

Before she could answer, he drew her in for a scandalous kiss right in the middle of the market. Ivy melted into him and responded on a primal level. She threw her arms around his neck and pressed her body into his.

After a few moments, he pulled away. "I think it's time for us to head back," he rasped. "I have plans for us which are best carried out behind closed doors. Unless—"

"No," she whispered. "Let's go back to my suite. I think we need some alone time."

"I couldn't have said it better myself." He took her arm, and they walked back to the taxi stand.

****

In the cab on the way back to the hotel, they couldn't keep their hands off each other. The friendly driver smiled and said, "Aloha. Are you two newlyweds?"

Ivy laughed and snuggled into the crook of Lucas's neck. She was suddenly embarrassed by their public displays of affection, but it didn't bother Lucas. Nevertheless, she hadn't regretted a moment.

"Umm, we are just a happy couple right now," Lucas answered for both of them. "But if we do get married, this is a great honeymoon destination."

"It sure is," the driver replied as he pulled up to the hotel entrance. "Be sure to come back and visit us again. Mahalo, and enjoy the rest of your holiday."

"Mahalo," Lucas said. "And yes, I think we make a pretty fantastic couple."

Ivy blushed at his bold statement, but she was secretly thrilled to hear Lucas speak of their relationship with such affection.

He paid the driver, thanked him, and then helped Ivy out of the taxi. She was brimming with desire for him and could tell by the way he was holding on to her that he had the same carnal thoughts. They reached her suite in mere minutes, and as the door closed behind them, they were alone again—in their own world.

Chapter Six

It was now early January, and Ivy and Lucas were back from their blissful, sun-filled vacation. They had experienced such a wonderful time—the best—and she had told him so often. But he was never tired of hearing it. He told her it was the first of many trips they would take to the beautiful island.

When they got back, Ben and his wife Karen invited them to dinner at their apartment on the outskirts of the city. This was a big step for Lucas, but he was ready. Since he was an only child, Ben was as close to a brother as Lucas could get, and his wife, Karen, was great, too. Always worried about Lucas, she was kind of like a big sister. Since Lucas's parents and most of his extended family lived in Florida, Ben and Karen were his only support in New York City. He appreciated them more than words could say, and they felt the same about him.

Ivy had been excited to meet them when he had told her about it. But as they made their way across town to Ben and Karen's in Lucas's jet-black classic car, she grabbed Lucas by the thigh.

"What if they don't like me, Lucas? What did you tell them about me? Do they think I'm a snob because I'm a motivational speaker?"

He put his hand on top of hers to soothe her. "Relax. They are going to love you. I've told Ben a lot about you. After all, we spend so many hours together when we are working. And I think he's pretty open with Karen, but everything I've said is good, I promise you. I couldn't think of a bad thought about you if I tried."

She pursed her lips at him. "Sure, sure. You're just trying to make me feel better."

"Well yes, but also, it's true." He smiled at her from the driver's seat. "Now, c'mon. It's going to be fun."

She hesitated before answering, "Okay. But just so you know, I'm paying you back for this. You are going to get to meet my sister very soon."

Lucas tried to be cool about meeting Jade. He had to admit to himself he was a little nervous, but he didn't want Ivy to know that. "Sounds good," he lied.

She smirked at him. "You have no idea what you are in for."

"Well, if she's anything like you, I already like her."

Lucas pulled into a parking spot near a beautiful brownstone. It was three stories tall, and Ivy admired the building. "This is nice," she said.

Lucas parked the car and took her hand. "Yeah, they have a great place on the second floor. Listen, Ivy," he said as he gazed at her with tenderness. "Just be your gorgeous self, and don't be nervous, okay?"

Before she could answer, he leaned over and pressed his lips to hers. He kissed her deeply, tasting the white wine she had been drinking before they left. It was intoxicating. No matter how often they were intimate, he always wanted more of her—like right now.

He broke contact with her and whispered in her

ear. "Let's just call it a night and go back to my place. I don't want to share you."

She frowned at him. "Lucas, we're here. We can't just leave."

"I guess you're right. But you're coming back to my place after, aren't you? I can't sleep anymore unless you are with me."

"I think you've got that backward, but yes. Unless you completely embarrass me tonight, you won't be sleeping alone."

He smiled and kissed her forehead. "Okay, let's get in there so we can leave sooner."

"Lucas, this was your idea, remember?"

"Yeah, I know. But that was before you curled your hair and put on that short skirt. Now I just want to undress you."

She smiled and shook her head at him. "You already did that, like half an hour ago."

"I know. But it was so much fun, I want to do it again."

She laughed. "Sometimes you are so weird. Grab the wine and the salad, and let's go meet your best friends."

"Okay, but when we get home, I'm going to peel that cute skirt and blouse right off your beautiful body—again." Without waiting for a reply, he ran over to the passenger side and helped her out of the car. Then he grabbed her hand, and they headed for the building.

****

When they reached the second floor, Lucas led Ivy down a short hallway. Before he could knock on apartment six, the door burst open. A woman of

97

average height with dark-brown hair cut in a sleek bob stood there with her hands on her hips. She was dressed in a pretty navy dress with yellow and gray accents, and her dark eyes were bright.

"Finally, you decide to show up," she admonished, giving Lucas a big hug. "Honestly, I don't know how you and Ben get your passengers anywhere on time. Do you ever look at your watch? You're always late."

Ivy gave Lucas a hard stare. He hadn't mentioned to her what time they were supposed to be there, and she thought they had been on schedule. Well, that was until she appeared before him at his condo in her short black skirt and pale-lavender silk blouse. He was looking handsome in dark-gray dress pants and a white button-down shirt. Then one thing had led to another, of course, since they couldn't keep their hands off each other. They ended up making love in the middle of Lucas's living room. And now, she supposed, they were officially late.

Before Lucas could respond to Karen's rhetorical question, she burst out laughing a singsong laugh which put Ivy at ease. "I'm just kidding. Ben's not even ready yet; he's still getting dressed. You boys," she said and winked at Ivy, "would be lost without us, right?"

Before she could respond, Karen enveloped Ivy in a warm hug. "I'm so glad to meet you. Please come in." She gestured the two of them inside. The foyer was an open concept, sharing the space with a large living room. It was done in rich brown tones with comfortable looking furniture and a big fireplace that had a roaring fire going in it. Ivy found it to be a charming, welcoming home. There were two hallways, one off to each side. She guessed one went to the kitchen and dining area and the other to the bedrooms.

"I'm very happy to meet you, too," Ivy said. She already liked Karen a lot.

Karen took their coats and led them to the sitting area. Lucas and Ivy sat down on the dark-chocolate sofa beside each other.

"Make yourselves at home," Karen said. "I'm just going to tell my husband to hurry up."

She dashed down the far hallway, her heels clicking on the wood floor as she walked away.

"Lucas," Ivy said when she thought Karen was out of earshot. "Are we really late? Because if so—"

Lucas didn't answer. Instead, he cut her off with an intense kiss that had her brain scrambling to remember what she was saying. She was swept away—her tongue finding his—and she touched his freshly shaven jaw. He reached for the buttons on her blouse, and she suddenly remembered where they were.

"Lucas, stop."

"Oh, don't worry," he said in his deep, seductive voice. "Karen will spend half an hour back there lecturing Ben about how he's never ready on time."

"I heard that," Karen said, coming back down the hall with Ben in tow.

Lucas smiled and moved his hand from her breast to her thigh. Ivy promptly grabbed it and set it between them. She gave Lucas a look. "We'll discuss this later." He just grinned back at her. Her stomach dropped at the sight of his megawatt smile with his full lips and perfect white teeth.

Lucas and Ivy stood up to greet Ben. He and Lucas exchanged a quick hug, and then Ben turned to Ivy. "Lucas," he said. "She's much more beautiful than you let on." He turned to Ivy. "It's a pleasure to finally meet you, Ivy. Trust me, he won't stop talking about you."

"It's good to meet you, too, Ben. I've heard a lot about you as well," Ivy said, and they exchanged a friendly embrace.

"Yes, well Lucas relies on me heavily at work. Did you know he can barely fly the plane without me? He's always like, 'what's this dial for again'?"

"Hardly," Lucas said and laughed. "It's the other way around, and you know it."

"Okay, boys," Karen interrupted. "No fighting in front of Ivy. She doesn't know us very well yet, and we want to make a good impression. Do I make myself clear?"

"Yes, dear," both Ben and Lucas said at the same time, and everyone laughed, even Ivy. She felt included in this tight-knit group already, and it was reassuring to her.

"Now," Karen said after everyone had quieted down. "How about some drinks and appetizers?"

The women had red wine and the men drank beer. They dined on fresh, raw vegetables with onion dip and a selection of exotic cheeses and crackers for starters. The conversation flowed easily, and Ivy could see why Lucas loved Karen and Ben. They were warm and made Ivy feel like part of the family. She was having a great time.

For dinner, they had butter chicken which Karen had prepared in the slow cooker. The chicken had been marinating in the spices all day, and it was divine. Naan bread and jasmine rice accompanied the meal. A green salad that Ivy had made topped off the selection. Ivy ate heartily and took pleasure in both the meal and the company. Lucas seemed to be enjoying himself as well. He stuck close to Ivy's side and kept checking in with her to make sure she was doing well. He held her hand all through dinner.

Ben and Karen held hands as well, so it didn't feel awkward. She could tell they were a happy couple, and they looked really cute together. Ben's fair complexion and reddish-brown hair were in sharp contrast to Karen's dark hair and eyes. Karen was of Indian descent and Ben had Irish roots; they made a stunning pair.

After dinner, Ivy offered to help Karen with the dishes, and the men went into the living room to talk business.

"Honestly," Karen said and laughed as they made their way into the kitchen with the plates. "They spend half their life flying together, and they still talk about it endlessly."

"Yes," Ivy agreed. "They are both really passionate about it."

Ivy looked around the spacious kitchen. It was done in a burnt orange with oak cupboards. Just like the rest of the space, Ivy thought it was inviting.

"Well, enough about them," Karen said and waved her hand around as she turned on the water to rinse the dishes. "Ivy, tell me, how are things going with Lucas?"

Normally, Ivy would be taken aback by someone she just met asking about her lover, but she felt comfortable with Karen and knew how much she cared about Lucas. They were as close as family, so she didn't mind sharing her thoughts with her. Besides, everything had been going so well, Ivy could hardly believe it.

"It's great," she said, smiling. "He's a wonderful guy. Sometimes I still feel like I don't deserve him."

"Yes, he is, but don't put yourself down. You're both great people who have been through a lot. I'm just glad you found each other," Karen said, her tone becoming serious. "And after his last girlfriend broke his heart, I wasn't sure he would ever try again, but I'm glad he did."

"Oh," Ivy said, surprised. "I never really asked him about his past girlfriends. What happened?"

"Well, he fell hard for her. And one day, Deanna just up and left him. He was devastated, to say the least." Karen seemed to suddenly realize she was overstepping a boundary. "But I really shouldn't be dredging up his past with you. What matters now is he has you, and you make a great couple."

Ivy smiled but felt guilty for not asking Lucas about his past. She had talked a lot about her late husband, Matt, when they had first gotten together, and Lucas had listened to every word. But he had never brought up his past relationships, so she just figured he didn't want to talk about it. But before Ivy could dwell on it too much longer, Karen changed the subject. "Would you like some coffee?"

Ivy said she would, and the two women sat at the lovely antique table and continued to chat like old friends. Ivy discovered Karen and Ben had been married for almost three years, and they desperately wanted a baby.

"Unfortunately, it's just not working out," Karen said. "We went through some pretty intense treatments, but they weren't effective. Now we want to adopt, but that's a long, difficult process as well. We've started, but I think we have a bumpy road ahead of us."

"I'm sorry to hear that," Ivy said. Ben and Karen were great together, and she could tell they would make wonderful parents. Life just wasn't fair sometimes, and she often struggled with this concept, especially where her work was concerned.

"Thank you. But don't worry; we haven't given up hope. We'll get there. It's just probably going to take longer than we thought."

Ivy reached over and took Karen's hand. "That's great. I'm glad to hear it."

Just then, Lucas and Ben came bustling into the kitchen, arguing about something regarding federal flying regulations.

"Enough shop talk," Karen said, smiling at the two men. Ivy could tell she spent a lot of time with Ben and Lucas together. She made a mental note to pick her brain some more the next time they got together.

"Let's have dessert," Karen said in a tone Ivy thought she used on the wayward teenagers she taught English to at the local high school.

The group returned to the living room, and they enjoyed homemade carrot cake and coffee. Lucas and Ben continued to argue, and Karen ran interference. It seemed like a pretty common pattern with these three, and Ivy enjoyed being pulled into the fold.

Later, while Ben and Karen were in the kitchen putting away the last of the dishes, Lucas leaned over and planted soft, intimate kisses on Ivy's neck. His goatee brushed against her skin, and she sighed at his gentle touch. "I think it's time to go," he whispered. "I've got plans for just the two of us."

She turned and looked into his stunning green eyes

which were brimming with desire for her. Ivy kissed his temple and whispered back, "I've had a fantastic time. But I think we could use some alone time as well."

They got up, and Lucas put a protective arm around her waist. Ben and Karen came walking out of the kitchen hand in hand.

"Are you finally going to rescue Ivy from us?" Ben said with a laugh.

"I had a marvelous time," Ivy said. "It's just I have an early meeting tomorrow, but thank you for a terrific evening."

They said their good-byes then, and Karen and Ivy made plans to have lunch. Lucas promised they would all get together again soon at his place. Then he whisked her away, back to his car, and across the city to his Manhattan condo.

****

One evening about a week after their dinner with Karen and Ben, Lucas and Ivy were sharing a relaxing meal at his place. Ivy had been staying there every night when he wasn't working, and he had encouraged her to leave some of her stuff there so it felt more like home. He had made room in the closet and cleaned out a drawer in his dresser for her.

The condo was decorated tastefully with white walls and comfortable leather furniture. Lucas was an amateur photographer, so pictures of his shots were blown up, framed, and displayed around the space. They were mostly scenes of the many places he had visited, but there were a few family shots as well.

The kitchen was spacious with quartz countertops and ebony cupboards. He had been constantly trying to make her feel comfortable, and it was working. She loved the fact he cared about her so much, even though she sometimes still felt like she didn't deserve this new chance at life.

They were finishing up dinner, a delicious a pecan-encrusted tilapia with risotto and grilled vegetables, Lucas had cooked for them. Was there anything this man couldn't do? Ivy was wistfully remembering the heat, sun, and sand of Hawaii. The weather had been nothing but snow since they had gotten back to New York City. Lucas was listening to her carry on when the doorbell rang.

"Who could that be?" Ivy inquired.

"Probably someone selling something. I'm not in the mood," he said as he got up from the table and made his way around to her. He scooped her up, and she threw her arms around his neck. "What I am in the mood for is you."

She laughed and tried to scold him. "Put me down. You can't ignore the door."

"Oh, yes I can." He moved out of the kitchen with her in his arms and into the living room.

"What if it's that package you have been waiting for?" She knew he was expecting some documents from work and didn't want him to miss the delivery.

"Oh yeah," he said, as he seemed to remember what she was talking about. He deposited her on the soft black leather couch and gave her a quick kiss. "Stay right here and don't move. I'll be back in a minute." She laughed at his comment and made herself comfortable to wait for him to return.

She watched his long, lean form stride down the hallway and marveled about how lucky she had been to find Lucas. He was an affectionate lover who cared for her in and out of the bedroom. His massive, king-size bed was where they had spent most of their time lately. She found that space calming and soothing, as it was done in various shades of gray. Ivy started to imagine what she was going to thrill him with tonight when the loud sound of a baby crying echoed from down the hallway. Who did he know that had a child?

Curious, she walked toward the entranceway. Lucas was standing there, looking tense and uncomfortable. He was staring at the gorgeous young woman who filled the doorway. She was petite and had an infant propped up on her hip. Her long, black hair reached her waist, and she was eyeing Lucas with big brown eyes. *Who is she?*

Ivy didn't want to eavesdrop, but she stood frozen on the spot, taking in the scene. Something was wrong. "Deanna, what are you doing here?" Lucas asked in a harsh tone. Ivy had never heard him speak like that. The woman seemed not to care.

"What's wrong, Lucas? Aren't you glad to see me?"

He narrowed his eyes and frowned at her. "No, I'm not. What do you want?"

She pouted. "Aren't you going to at least invite me in?"

Lucas seemed to hesitate, and he turned to see Ivy standing there. She found her voice. "What's going on, Lucas?"

"Ivy," he breathed, looking more upset than she had ever seen him. "This is Deanna, an old friend. She was just leaving."

"No, I'm not," the ebony-haired beauty interrupted. She gave Ivy a once over and then dismissed her. Her gaze wandered back to Lucas. "We need to talk—alone."

He stood firmly in her way, not giving in.

"Okay," he finally said. "Say what you need to say, Deanna. This is Ivy, my girlfriend." He gestured in Ivy's direction but wouldn't look her in the eye. "Anything you need to tell me you can say in front of her."

The woman's eyes gave away her surprise, but she didn't challenge Lucas further.

"Fine," she said and held the baby out to Lucas. "Here." She tried to hand the infant to Lucas, but he backed away from her.

"What's the matter, Lucas? Don't you want to hold your son?"

Ivy reeled back, grabbing the wall for support. She felt faint, and her eyes began to fill with tears. *Lucas has a baby with this woman? No, this can't be happening.*

Lucas's voice rose with anger. "I don't have a son with you, Deanna. You're lying."

She shook her long mane of hair at him. "No, I'm not. Now let me in, and I'll show you the proof."

Ivy glanced at the baby. He had gorgeous green eyes and light hair, but he couldn't be Lucas's. *Could he?*

Panic rose in her chest. She had to get out of there—now.

She retrieved her coat and purse from the hall closet. "I must leave," she stammered more to herself than anyone else.

Lucas was at her side in a flash. "No, Ivy. Don't go. Stay."

His voice was imploring her, but she ignored it. A pain swept through her chest, and one glance at Deanna told her the woman was pleased with what was happening.

Trying not to make this nightmare any more horrible than it already was, she put on her coat and then looked at Lucas. "No. You've got some things to discuss with your old friend, and I'll just get in the way. Goodbye, Lucas."

She headed for the door, ignoring his protests. Choosing the stairs instead of the elevator, she made her way down to the ground level. She sprinted for the exit and found herself engulfed in a freezing cold snowstorm that was taking over the city.

Ivy didn't feel the cold at all. Nevertheless, she reached into her purse for her gloves. As she searched for them, she noticed she didn't have the keys to her apartment. Great. She must have left them on the table in Lucas's entryway. Well, she wasn't going back for them, that was for sure. She'd just have to ask the doorman to let her into her apartment, and she would deal with her missing keys later.

Trudging through the snow, she felt hollow and empty inside. Had she lost Lucas to that woman and baby when they had just found each other? She had taken a chance on love and had a sinking feeling that she had failed, again.

****

Lucas was on the verge of an intense rage. How dare Deanna come back here and start accusing him of fathering a child with her. It just wasn't possible. He couldn't get the look of Ivy's hurt and betrayal out of his mind.

Now they were standing in the hallway, glaring at each other. Not wanting to disturb his neighbors, Lucas let Deanna into the condo. She looked pleased, and it fueled his anger even more. He would listen to her pathetic attempts to involve him in this mess, then he would get rid of her and go after Ivy.

Deanna made herself comfortable on Lucas's sofa and ignored his glares. The baby started to fuss. This whole thing was giving Lucas a migraine.

"Okay," he said when she was seated. "Tell me what you came here to say."

"Just a minute. Little Ryan is hungry. I'll just take care of that, and then we can talk."

And before Lucas could protest, she took off her top, exposing her breasts, and then began to feed the baby. *You've got to be kidding me.* Lucas looked away, embarrassed she was making such a scene. He moved into the kitchen to avoid seeing her and tried to calm himself down. No sense yelling and screaming at her. It would upset the baby and delay this horror show of hers. Although he knew it would be difficult, he had to stay neutral. He wasn't going to let her get under his skin.

He grabbed the bottle of whiskey he kept in the cupboard and poured himself a shot. Swallowing the strong alcohol without really tasting it, he took a few deep breaths. Then he made his way back out to the living room.

Deanna was propped up on the couch, looking smug. She had put her top on—thank goodness—and the now sleeping infant was in her arms.

"Shh," she said. "Don't wake him up." She pulled a blanket from her bag and spread it out on the carpet.

Lucas didn't move to help her. He wasn't going to encourage her getting any more comfortable than she already was.

She set the sleeping child down on the blanket and turned back to him.

"Ryan is yours, Lucas. You can't deny it. He's three months old, and we broke up ten months ago before I knew I was pregnant."

"That doesn't prove anything. I was pretty sure you were seeing someone else before you left me. Besides, if he's really mine, why didn't you contact me when this happened?"

"There was no one else, Lucas. I was scared and confused when I found out I was pregnant. Since we had already broken up, I moved back home to Kentucky to stay with my parents. They've been harassing me to tell you. Mom and Dad don't want to support us anymore, so I'm coming back to New York. I thought we could pick up where we left off. We just have a small addition to contend with."

He narrowed his eyes at her. "Well, you thought wrong. I'm with Ivy now, and I'm not taking your word for it. I want a paternity test."

She nodded. "I knew you would. I've set it all up on my end." She handed him some papers.

He glanced at them, but he was having trouble concentrating.

"Go to the lab listed on the paperwork, and they will take your blood. The results will be ready in about a week. Do you still think I'm lying, Lucas?"

"I don't know…" He was so confused right now.

"I wouldn't have arranged this unless I knew he was your child." She glanced from Lucas to the baby and back as if to prove her point.

He let out a long sigh. "I'm not going to believe what you are saying until I have proof. Let's see what the tests say, and then we will discuss it. Now, it's time for you to leave."

Deanna didn't move. She just sat across from him, staring. When he didn't say anything, she broke the silence. "I was hoping Ryan and I could stay here. The hotel we are staying at is expensive and not a home, like here."

Lucas groaned. There was no way she's staying here. This was all a big lie. Yet he didn't feel quite as convinced as he had been earlier.

He reached into his back pocket and pulled out his wallet. Taking out several hundred-dollar bills, he handed them to her. She smiled sweetly at him, and he felt sick to his stomach.

"Trying to buy me off already, Lucas?"

"Get out, Deanna. And I don't want to see or hear from you until the paternity test comes back."

"Very well," she said. "But if you change your mind and want to spend some quality time with your son, give me a call." She handed him a piece of paper with her phone number on it. He tossed it on the coffee table. His anger was on the verge of erupting again.

"Leave now, Deanna, before I throw you out."

"Okay, okay," she replied and got up. Lucas watched as she gathered her things and scooped up the still sleeping child. He moved with her toward the door as he couldn't wait to be rid of her. Lucas opened the door, and she stepped outside. He was just closing it in her face when she spoke. "See you soon, Daddy."

He cursed and slammed the door. Lucas was so

angry, he thought he might do something crazy. Thankfully, he spied Ivy's keys on the table by the door, and it distracted him from his murderous thoughts. He had to go to her to hold her and tell her everything was going to be okay. But was it? It didn't matter. All that mattered was Ivy, and he had to be there for her. He was worried she would have a nightmare due to all the stress, so he grabbed his coat from the closet and took off to find her.

Twenty minutes later, he had taken a taxi the few short blocks to her apartment. He let himself in with her keys. It was dark and quiet. She was probably sleeping, given the late hour. He crept into her bedroom and shrugged out of his clothes as he took in the sight of her sleeping form. From the moonlight filtering through the curtains, he could see that a frown marred her beautiful face, and she had been crying. This was all his fault. He had to make it up to her, somehow.

****

Ivy felt like she was in a haze, somewhere between sleep and consciousness. She was tired but also upset. Her foggy brain couldn't remember what, so she tried to go back to sleep. The bed creaked and warm, strong arms encircled her waist. Lucas. He was here. He pulled her close to his bare chest, and she inhaled his white musk scent. It instantly relaxed her. She struggled to open her eyes and sit up.

"Shh," he whispered into the darkness. "Just sleep now."

She turned to him and as her lips found his, she tried to recall what was going on. Instead, she was swept up into a passion-filled kiss by her sensuous lover. Everything else faded into the background and she deepened the contact, tasting whiskey on his tongue.

She reached down, and after pulling down his boxers, she stroked his manhood. He groaned and tugged off her nightshirt. She was now naked beneath him, and he kissed her breasts, her stomach, and then moved lower. He was driving her to the edge.

She pulled his face up to meet hers, and he plunged into her. His toned body hovered above her as he moved in and out of her, slowly. She grabbed his hips and increased the tempo. That brought her to the edge. A few more thrusts had her crying out in an earth-shattering climax. He followed soon after that, grunting out his raw need for her.

He collapsed beside her on the bed, panting. Lucas pulled her on top of him in a tight embrace. She snuggled into his warmth. He wrapped the blankets around them. Ivy was dozing off again, feeling safe and secure in Lucas's protective arms.

Suddenly, a shiver of dread ran through her. Something had happened. Her mind flashed back to the scene at his condo and her head shot up in alarm, as her eyes flew open. "Lucas," she said, her voice filled with panic. "That woman. She came to your place with a baby and said it was yours. You have to break up with me."

He gazed at her with heartfelt emotion etched on his gorgeous face. "That's not going to happen. Now you need to get some sleep. I don't want your nightmares starting again. We can talk about it in the morning."

"No…" She tried to protest.

"Hey, you're here with me now. Safe. Close your

eyes. All that nonsense can wait."

Lucas planted little kisses on her face and neck, and she lay back down on his sculpted chest. He stroked her hair and back. She slowly drifted off to sleep but as she did, a river of tears slid silently down her cheeks.

****

Ivy awoke late the next morning and felt like she had a massive hangover, but she couldn't remember drinking last night. The sound of Lucas clattering about in the kitchen had her smiling. Then her smile faded as it dawned on her. The memory of last night's events rushed through her, and she didn't want to face him. Because if she did, it would be over between them. If Lucas had fathered a child with another woman—one who clearly wanted him back, she wouldn't be able to get past that fact.

She remembered what Karen had said about how heartbroken Lucas had been when Deanna left him. Ivy wouldn't fight against this obstacle. After what had happened with Matt, she didn't think she had it in her for a battle the likes of this one. And besides, if she had to struggle to hang onto Lucas, it would only end in disaster for her. Ivy decided she would just give him up; it was better for everyone involved.

She sighed, pulled up the covers over her head, and tried to go back to sleep. Maybe Lucas would just leave, and then they wouldn't have to get into it. Then she could forgo the devastating conversation that would end their love affair after it had only just begun. The weight of her grief made her eyes heavy, so she closed them. She was just drifting off again when he entered her bedroom.

She could smell the freshly brewed coffee he brought with him. Hearing him set it down on the nightstand and sit on the bed, she turned to him but didn't open her eyes.

"Ivy," he whispered. "I'm sorry to wake you up, but I have to leave soon for work. I have a cross-country flight and will be gone for a couple of days. We need to talk before I go."

Her stomach dropped at the sound of his deep, seductive voice—one that would soon tell her good-bye.

She opened her eyes and peered at him. Concern was engraved on his face. He looked like he hadn't slept much. Lucas was trying to smile at her, but the gesture didn't reach his eyes. She'd better get this over with. It was time.

"Okay. Just let me have a quick shower, and I'll meet you in the kitchen."

He reached for her and she pulled away. "Lucas, don't," she said and made her way into the bathroom.

Ten minutes later, she was dressed in black yoga pants and a heavy, comfortable gray sweater. *I'll have to keep myself warm from now on.* Her body let out an involuntary shiver as if it was trying to remind her of that fact. She padded into the kitchen barefoot and stared at Lucas. He was dressed in his rumpled clothes from the night before and a shadow lined his jaw. There were dark circles under his beautiful eyes, and she had to restrain herself from going to him. She watched him as he stared into his coffee, an anguished expression on his face.

He stood when she approached him and he rushed to hand her the coffee, already laden with cream and sugar. She accepted it without comment and sat down at the table.

Dropping into the seat across from her, Lucas reached for her hand, but she moved it out of his grasp. "Please," she whispered. "Don't make this harder than it already is."

Lucas tried to catch her eye, but she looked away. If she didn't, he would see the words she spoke were not at all in alignment with her emotions. She was going to tell him to leave, even though her heart was begging her to make him stay. But she was determined her rational side would win this time, so she hid her gaze.

When she said nothing to him for several moments, he spoke. "It's not hard, Ivy. Nothing has changed. I'm not going to break up with you over this."

Ivy sighed and knew she had to say the words that would divide them forever. She could barely make herself do it, and then she did. "Well, then I'll have to break up with you."

He let out a cry of frustration, but she ignored him.

Before she could stop herself, she blurted out her questions. Ones she already knew the answers to, but she wanted to hear him say it. It would make what she had to do easier. "Who is she, Lucas? What did she say? Tell me the truth."

He raked his hands through his already messy hair. "She's just an old girlfriend, Deanna Mason. We broke up almost a year ago, and I haven't heard from her since. Then she shows up at my door with this kid and says it's mine. But she's lying, Ivy. It can't be. I'm going to get a paternity test. Here, I've already got the papers. Deanna set it up to try and trick me into not getting one. But I'm going through with it, and I'm not the father."

Ivy took the papers he was holding out to her across the table. Yes, it looked like a requisition for a blood test. But did that even matter? It didn't. And she wasn't sure she shared Lucas's conviction.

"How can you be certain? The baby is gorgeous and looks just like you."

He frowned and it just added to his exhausted look. "No, that's not true. I'm not going to let this separate us."

She handed the papers back to him and said in a slow and steady voice. "It already has."

"No," he shouted as he got up and made his way over to her. Ivy got up from the table and backed away from him. She had gained control of her emotions, but one touch from him would cause everything to come crashing down around her.

"Yes, Lucas," she said with a cool and detached tone. "And we shouldn't have been together last night."

"Hey," he said, trying to catch her eye again. This time she looked at him. She saw a look of devotion in his eyes, one that she was sure mirrored hers. With emotion heavy in his voice, he spoke. "Last night wasn't a mistake for me. The only mistake we are making is letting this come between us."

She looked away from his intense gaze, sighed, and sat down again. She was exhausted and heartsick. *I have to do this now, or I'll fall apart right in front of him.*

"It's time for you to go, Lucas. I'm going to need some space. Please respect my wishes."

She could feel his stare burning into her, but she

didn't look up.

"This isn't the end of us, Ivy. I'll give you some distance while I'm working, but as soon as I'm back in the city, you will see me again."

He didn't give her a chance to reply as he stormed out of the kitchen. A moment later, the front door slammed, and she collapsed on her kitchen floor, sobbing. Ivy lay there for the longest time, feeling broken apart because she had just found her soulmate. But now, it appeared he was lost to her—forever.

Chapter Seven

Lucas was a complete wreck on the flight from New York to Los Angeles. Thank goodness for Ben, as he pretty much took over for him. He was an experienced pilot himself and could easily have become captain, but he said he'd never find a better partner or friend than Lucas, so they stuck together. Lucas didn't often let him take the reins, but with the stress of the past twenty-four hours and his total lack of sleep last night, he acquiesced.

He told Ben the entire story as they flew across the country. Deanna showing up, Ivy leaving, and then Lucas going to her apartment. He had spent the entire night watching Ivy and running through the complete wreck that had become his life in his head. Thank goodness Ivy hadn't had a nightmare. But their fight this morning had just added to his stress. Lucas was worried about Ivy and felt he was one step away from falling apart completely. As usual, Ben was both sympathetic and realistic.

"Hey, man," he said. "You can't get all worked up about this until you know all the facts."

"I know, you're right," Lucas said. "I just can't help but think this whole situation has driven a wedge between Ivy and me. I mean, she's already been through so much in her past, she doesn't need mine coming back to haunt us."

Ben cocked his head to one side, a thoughtful expression on his face. "Listen, from what you've told me, Ivy is a strong, courageous lady. Otherwise, how could she put up with you?"

Lucas groaned. He knew Ben was just trying to cheer him up, but he wasn't in the mood.

"Hey, just kidding, buddy. But I think she really is—maybe more than you know. Give her some credit, Lucas. I know you want to look after her and protect her from everything, but that's not always possible. Besides, Deanna could be making this whole thing up to cause trouble for you or to try and get you back. Don't give her the satisfaction."

At the mention of his ex-girlfriend's name, Lucas felt his blood pressure rise and the dull headache he had been dealing with all day intensify. But Ben was right. She didn't deserve a second of his time unless—well, he didn't want to think about that possibility.

"You're right, again."

Ben smiled. "I know. But I never tire of hearing you say it." He laughed. "But seriously, why don't you go in the back and take a quick nap? First class is almost empty. I love you, man, but you look like hell. I promise I'll come and get you if anything happens, but it looks like smooth sailing to California."

"Yeah, okay. Thanks, Ben. I owe you one."

"Don't worry about it. Now go."

Lucas walked to the back of the deserted first-class section. He sank into a comfortable leather chair and closed his eyes. But sleep wouldn't come—only more disturbing thoughts.

Had he ever had unprotected sex with Deanna when they were together? He was almost one hundred percent certain they hadn't. Because, although he had been infatuated with her, something inside him hadn't totally trusted her. She said she was clean, but she had boasted about having more lovers than she could count. Lucas had found her proclamation odd and was sure he hadn't taken any chances. He had used a condom every time. Still, it was possible they hadn't worked.

Earlier on the way to the airport, he had stopped by the clinic and had the required blood test. The paternity results couldn't come soon enough for him. Unfortunately, he still had about a week to wait. The lab said they would call him as soon as they had an answer. This thought gave him little comfort.

And Lucas still had a nagging feeling Deanna had been involved with someone else near the end of their relationship. Then she just disappeared. He was upset at first, but then later, he found he didn't really miss her. This had been further proof they weren't a good match. But he and Ivy were a perfect match, and he was going to tell her that as soon as he got home.

He just hoped she would be more willing to listen to him than she had been this morning. Lucas hated the way they had left things, but he could tell Ivy wasn't in the mood to work it out, and nothing he said or did could change that right now. But perhaps after she had some time to think, he could get through to her. Clinging to that thought, he drifted into an uneasy sleep and had a terrible vision of Ivy moving on—without him.

****

Ivy spent the next week dissolving into tears every five seconds. She couldn't concentrate on work, or anything else, for that matter. She had been avoiding

Lucas's constant texts and calls. It was painful to do so, but she felt she had no choice. There was no way she was going to be caught in the middle of this. If Lucas was a father, he needed to concentrate on that, not her. And well, if he wasn't, he needed to deal with Deanna once and for all before she would talk to him.

Finally, after this had been going on for about a week, Jade showed up at her door and let herself in. Ivy was lying on the couch, watching mindless morning television, and she wasn't planning on moving all day, if possible. Jade let out a gasp when she saw her.

"Ivy," she crooned and made her way over to the couch. "Why didn't you tell me to come over? It's much worse than you said on the phone."

She shrugged. "I'm sorry. It's just you are so busy with work, and I didn't want to bother you. Besides, I'm fine, really."

Jade enveloped Ivy in a warm hug, and she began to cry.

"Shh," her sister soothed. "You are not fine, but I'm here now. You said you and Lucas broke up, but this is more than that. Tell me what happened."

Ivy recounted the horrible events of the past week as Jade listened in her usual intense manner. When Ivy had finished her story, Jade fired off questions in her no-nonsense tone. "Who is this woman? What's her history?"

"Oh, don't start with that, detective sister. Lucas admits they had a relationship, so she could have had his child."

Jade narrowed her eyes. "Okay, but something isn't sitting right with me."

"Drop it. I'm having a hard enough time with this

without you snooping around."

"Fine," Jade said in a tone that meant she was up to something. But Ivy was too tired and upset to care.

"Now, go get cleaned up. We are going out for breakfast."

Ivy sighed. "No, Jade, I'm really not up to it."

Jade shook her head. "I've let you wallow in your misery long enough. Now get going."

"Okay," Ivy replied weakly and went to stand up. There was no point arguing with Jade when she was in one of her moods. When Ivy stood, she swayed a little on her feet, and Jade jumped up to grab her.

"Ivy," she admonished. "Have you been taking your blood pressure medication? And when was the last time you ate?"

"No, and I'm not hungry."

"Listen," Jade said in a harsh tone. "You have to take care of yourself. Now go take your medicine, and then we are going to go out for a huge meal."

Ivy didn't respond, just went into her bedroom to shower and dress.

An hour later, they were sitting at their favorite all-day breakfast place, and Ivy was stuffed. Although she had said she wasn't hungry to her sister, Jade knew she couldn't resist the banana chocolate-chip pancakes, so she had placed two orders. Ivy was glad she was wearing her comfortable yoga pants and a loose, pink sweater. Her hair was freshly washed, and she had put on a bit of makeup just to appease her nagging sister.

Ivy ate her share of the fluffy carbohydrates and then leaned back and sipped her coffee. She tried to smile at her sister. "See, I'm fine."

"I'm not totally convinced, but it's a start."

"Don't worry, I'll be okay. Besides, I have to go to Boston next week for a conference, so that will be a good distraction. Can you water my plants while I'm away? I'll be gone for three days, and the ferns won't last."

Jade nodded. "Sure, no problem. But hey, are you going to talk to Lucas?"

"Not yet. I'm just not ready."

"Why?"

"Jade, please," Ivy said shaking her head. "I'm pretty sure he's fathered a child with another woman—one he may have never gotten over. I just can't be in the middle of that mess right now. It's all too much."

"Fine," Jade said in a tone that told Ivy her heartfelt speech had little impact. "But maybe he didn't, and maybe he's totally over her. Did you ever think about that?"

"Of course. But there's just so much that's unknown right now. Once I have some facts, I'll talk to him. Please, tell me you can understand that."

"Yes, I understand. Okay, little sister. You look marginally better, and I hate to do this, but I gotta run. Duty calls. Are you sure you're all right?"

"Yes, I'm fine. Go and save the world. I'll call you when I get back from my trip."

Jade smiled and got up to give Ivy a hug. Ivy tried her best not to start crying again.

"Love you, Ivy. Have a safe trip."

"I love you, too, now go."

Jade bounded off and Ivy watched her leave. She finished her coffee and then took a walk. It was the first time she had left her apartment in days, and she needed to clear her head and work off those pancakes.

Twenty minutes later, she found herself outside of Lucas's downtown condo. *How did I end up here?* She had been walking aimlessly, not really paying attention to where she was going. Her heart ached to see him, but her mind just wasn't ready. She quickly turned to leave and walk back to her place, when she saw him exit the front door of his building.

He was dressed casually in jeans and a wool jacket looking as handsome as ever, but he had a serious expression on his face she rarely saw. She turned away from him, trying to flee without him noticing her, but it was too late. He had seen her.

"Ivy," he called and broke into a run. When he reached her, he put his hands in his pockets, looking awkward and uncomfortable. "How are you?"

"I'm fine," she said, trying to sound braver than she felt.

His face softened into a look she knew all too well. "Hey," he said. "You don't have to pretend with me."

A tear slid down her cheek, and he held out his arms to her. She silenced her rational mind as she walked into his embrace. He smelled of white musk and soap, and she relaxed in his grasp. She leaned her head on his shoulder and savored this intimate moment, right in the middle of downtown Manhattan. People hustled and bustled around them.

"I've been calling and texting you," he whispered in her ear. His tone became melancholy. "I thought you didn't want to see me."

"I'm sorry, Lucas," Ivy murmured through tears, which were now streaming down her face.

"You don't have to be sorry. This situation has been difficult for both of us. C'mon, let's go upstairs and talk."

"Weren't you on your way out?" she asked, no longer certain she wanted to face him again.

"I was just headed to the store. Nothing I can't do later." He seemed to notice her hesitation. "Would you rather grab a coffee somewhere?"

She thought for a moment, then decided this was not a discussion she wanted to have in public. "No, let's go up to your place."

He smiled his gorgeous smile, put his arm around her, and led her back up to his condo.

****

Lucas was relieved—but also extremely nervous—to see Ivy again. She looked beautiful and was dressed in a casual, long, black winter coat with an enormous green scarf. But he could see the strain on her face and knew he was the cause of it. That thought made his heart ache. If only he could rewind the events of the past few weeks and give her back the carefree smile she had in Hawaii. Well, this nightmare would soon be over when he got the results of the paternity test. In the meantime, he just had to convince her to hang on and trust him.

He put a protective arm around her and pulled her close as they rode the elevator to his condo in silence. She smelled of fresh roses, and he inhaled her scent. *God, I miss that. I miss her.* When they reached his front door, he unlocked it and ushered her inside. The door shut behind them, and he turned to offer to take her jacket.

Instead, he saw a look in her eye he had never seen before. It was an expression of pure, raw need, and before he could question her, she grabbed him by the collar and pulled him into a passionate kiss.

He responded, pushed her back against the wall, and kissed her back with just as much desire. His tongue found hers, and he tasted strong coffee. Then he cupped the back of her neck and deepened their contact. He shrugged out of his jacket and helped her as she unzipped hers. They were haphazardly thrown to the floor. She tore at the buttons of his plaid shirt, and he ripped it off. He removed her sweater and threw it on the pile.

Hastily, they both removed their pants. Lucas was so caught up in the moment, he lost all form of rational thought. All he could think about was being inside Ivy—now. He stood naked in his front hall and turned her around. All of his muscles were rigid with his unbridled urge for her. Carefully removing her panties, he ran his hands down the length of her body. She shivered with yearning and now wore only a camisole. He ran kisses down the side of her neck and reached for the straps.

She turned back around before he could get a hold of them, once again facing him. Ivy grabbed his shoulders, lifted her legs, and wrapped them around his waist. He grasped her backside, supporting her with his biceps, and then he thrust into her, crying out when she enveloped him in her warm folds.

They moved at a rapid, fervid pace as if this highly intimate act could erase the space that had grown between them. An instant later, he came, shouting out in ecstasy. She seemed to be undone by his reaction and climaxed seconds after him, panting. Then she sagged against him.

He caught his breath, still supporting her form

tightly wrapped around him. Then he carried her into the bedroom and made love to her again—this time, at a slow and sensuous pace which lasted for the entire afternoon.

****

Dusk was just beginning to set a few hours later, and Lucas was dozing softly beside Ivy. She was wrapped in his arms and finally looked peaceful and content. He had been watching her for the past hour as she slept.

They hadn't really talked yet, but for now, he thought it was for the best. Being next to her in bed was more comforting than any words that could be spoken between them. And she needed her rest. There were dark circles shadowing her eyes when he saw her downstairs, and he vowed to help erase them. Not to mention the fact that he had wanted to eradicate the pain he saw in her eyes. He had done his best, he had been an attentive lover that afternoon. Besides, they could talk over dinner later, but in the meantime, he would let her sleep. He finally lay down on the pillow beside her, closed his eyes, and drifted off.

Moments after Lucas had fallen asleep, the loud shrill of his cell phone on the nightstand awoke him. He swore and grabbed it, glancing over at Ivy. She stirred but didn't wake. He moved out into the hallway to answer the call, shutting the door behind him. Jabbing at the accept button he grunted into the phone. "Freeman."

"Lucas Freeman?" The voice on the other end of the inquired. He didn't recognize it.

"Yes."

"This is Carol calling from Horizon Health Labs.

We have the results of your paternity test."

Lucas sucked in a breath and ran a shaky hand through his hair. This was the moment he had been waiting for. It would all be over soon. "Great. Yes, please tell me."

"The tests have confirmed you are a positive match to the child, Ryan Mason. You're the father of the baby in question."

"No," Lucas yelled into the phone before he could stop himself. He took a deep breath and tried to regain his composure. "There must be some mistake."

"I'm afraid not, sir," the woman replied. "Our results are conclusive. We can email you a breakdown of the tests if you need the paperwork."

"Yes, please do so," he said and then hung up on her, lest he let his barely unchecked rage surface again.

Sinking to the floor in his hallway, he dropped the phone and raked his hands through his hair. He refused to believe what he had just heard.

Wanting more proof, he ran into the living room where his laptop lay on the sofa. He booted it up and keyed in the password for his email account. The email from the lab popped up on his screen and he scrolled through it. It just confirmed his worst fear. He had fathered a child with Deanna. *What the hell am I going to do now?*

He couldn't tell Ivy. Lucas felt like he had just gotten her back, and now he would lose her again. But how could he hide this from her? He wouldn't. But it could wait till later. He would let her sleep and make some dinner for them. Then he would bare his soul to her and hope it was enough to keep her in his arms.

Lucas showered and dressed in track pants and a

gray t-shirt. His bare feet padded around the kitchen as he tried to be as quiet as possible. After he poured himself a few stiff drinks of single malt scotch, he began to relax as the alcohol had a numbing effect on his nerves. He didn't have much to eat at his place; he had been on his way to the supermarket when he saw Ivy standing outside his building.

And his condo was a disaster. He had gotten back the previous day from a round-trip flight to Atlanta, so he didn't have time to tidy up. Not that he had cared since Ivy had been avoiding contact with him. But now she was here. He hastily made his way around the living room, picking up clothes and take-out containers strewn around the space. When he was satisfied with his work, he tackled the mountain of dishes in his kitchen.

Lucas wanted to prepare a homemade pizza for the two of them for dinner. He always had those ingredients on hand. Not the most romantic dinner, but it would have to do. He wasn't going to leave Ivy alone, even if it were just to run to the store for a few minutes. He whipped up the dough and then covered it with sauce and toppings. The task gave his nervous hands something to do, and he began to relax a bit more.

The shower turned on, which told him Ivy was up. He put the pizza in the oven, tossed a garden salad, and poured her a glass of wine. Then he silently rehearsed what he was going to say to her.

Twenty minutes later, Ivy made her way into the kitchen, and Lucas smiled when he saw she was dressed in one of his plaid shirts with her yoga pants. Her hair was freshly brushed and hanging down her back, and she still had that sleepy, dreamy-eyed look in her violet-blue eyes.

"Why is your bed so much more comfortable than mine? I had a fantastic sleep," she said as she walked into his open arms.

"Oh, I don't know," he said, putting his arms around her and stroking her silky hair. "I think it's the company that makes all the difference."

"Maybe," she said, laughing, and snuggled deeper into his embrace.

"But I'm glad you had a good rest. You didn't need to get up; I would have brought you dinner in bed."

"I missed you. And besides, I thought we came up here to talk."

"We did, that is, until you took advantage of me in my front hallway."

"Oh, please." She laughed again, that soft, musical sound he never tired of hearing. "You loved every minute of it and you know it."

"I did. I'm not going to lie." He leaned down and kissed her passionately. She fisted her hands in his hair, and he groaned. *I want her, again.* But no, they had to have something to eat and then talk.

He pulled away. "If you keep this up, I'm going to burn your dinner."

She smiled. "Well, don't do that. I'm starved." He was glad to hear it. Lucas could tell she had lost some weight, and he felt another pang of guilt he was the cause of that, too. He handed her a glass of white wine.

"Okay, just a few more minutes and it will be ready. Let's go sit down."

He took her hand and led her into the living room. She sat down beside him on the couch and looked deep into his eyes.

"I can't stay away from you, Lucas. I tried and failed. I was just out walking today and found myself here."

"Good. I don't want you to. You need to stay right here…with me." He paused, took a deep breath, and then he said the words he had been thinking since the day he laid eyes on her for the first time. "Ivy, I love you, and I can't live without you."

"Oh, Lucas," she replied as her eyes filled with tears. "I love you, too."

"That's all that matters, Ivy. If we love each other, we can get through anything together."

She frowned. "I'm afraid it might not be enough this time. Have you heard anything about the paternity test?"

It was truth time. But his heart was heavy with the consequences of his revelation. "Yes," he said. "They called while you were sleeping."

"It isn't good news, is it? Otherwise, you would have told me already." She suddenly sounded strange and detached, and it filled him with dread.

"No. They said I'm the father of Deanna's baby. I'm so sorry, Ivy. I've prayed every day this situation wouldn't come to pass, but it has."

"Well," she said, standing up and letting his hand go. "I guess that's it. You've got a lot to deal with right now, and I can't be a part of that. Now I'm the one who's sorry, Lucas. Goodbye."

He was stunned into shocked silence and wanted to go after her. Yet, Lucas remained where he was frozen on the spot. Declaring his undying love for her hadn't been enough to save their relationship. He had given her everything he had, and despite that fact, it was still going to end in disaster.

As she walked into the hallway and retrieved her coat, a huge void opened inside him, and he doubted he would ever be whole again. The front door closed quietly, and she was gone. He leaned over, put his head in his hands, and cried.

A few moments later, a knock sounded at the door. He leaped up. It was Ivy. She had changed her mind and come back. He rushed into the hallway and threw open the door. Deanna stood there, looking just how she had over a week ago. The baby was sleeping in a carrier attached to her chest, and she had a smug look on her face. "Hi, Daddy," she crooned. "We're home."

Chapter Eight

Lucas stared at her, not really seeing anything. His mind was confused and his heart was aching. Deanna was the last person he wanted to see right now, but he had to face reality—his new reality without Ivy. And it wasn't fair to this innocent child to ignore the situation any longer.

He ushered her inside without comment, but she didn't seem to notice his mood as a steady stream of conversation flowed out of her. "So I guess you heard the good news. You're a father. Isn't that exciting, Lucas? I'm so glad we could work things out. The doorman is bringing up our stuff. I'm assuming we can stay here now. After all, we're officially a family."

Lucas finally found his voice. "You can stay here for a while, but you're going to have to look for your own place soon."

"What? Why? Oh, never mind. We can work out the details later."

Just then the doorbell rang, and Lucas went to retrieve her belongings. He carried in her three suitcases, traveling crib, and a stroller. After he put everything in his spare room, he went into the kitchen. Lucas removed the burnt pizza from the oven and threw it in the garbage. His appetite was gone. He took a few shots of scotch straight out of the bottle, then poured himself a hefty glass before he went back to face

Deanna.

She was seated on the sofa, looking happy and relaxed. It should bother him, but he was totally numb—to pain, to her, to everything. The baby was awake and sitting in her lap. He sat down across from her.

"Do you want to hold him, Lucas?"

"Um, I guess," he replied. He had never held a baby, and Deanna sensed his hesitation.

"He won't bite, I promise." She carried the infant over to him and sat down beside Lucas. When she gingerly placed the baby in his arms, she hovered with her hand on his bicep.

The baby stared up at Lucas with a wide-eyed, innocent expression. He found this whole situation surreal.

"Isn't he beautiful? And he looks just like you." He had to agree there was a striking resemblance, but he wasn't going to admit that to her.

A few minutes later, the baby started to fuss. He looked at Deanna in terror, unsure as to what to do. She took the baby out of his arms. "Oh, don't worry. I know you are new at this, but you'll be a pro in no time. He's just hungry."

Lucas took this opportunity to make a hasty exit.

"Okay, well your room is all set up. I'm going to bed. I have to get up early for a morning flight, so make yourself comfortable." *She already has, you don't have to remind her.*

"Thanks, Lucas. You are so sweet. I knew you'd come around eventually."

He didn't dignify that with an answer but just stomped off to bed.

Lucas fell asleep as soon as his head hit the pillow. The scotch had worked its magic and put him under quickly. He awoke to a strange sound later that night but he couldn't place it; his brain was still foggy from the alcohol.

Slender arms reached for him, and delicate hands caressed his bare chest. Ivy. She had come back to him. He pulled her toward him for a kiss, and big, full lips met his. Wait. Something was wrong. His eyes flew open, and in the semi-darkness he could see Deanna straddling him, naked. He quickly moved out of her grasp and switched on the bedside lamp.

"Deanna," he groaned, all remnants of sleep gone. "What are you doing?"

"Oh, c'mon, Lucas," she purred. "You know you want me. I still have this hot body you used to worship." She ran her hands suggestively over her breasts and down her torso.

Lucas audibly gasped in surprise and horror. *This can't be happening to me.* Then he found his voice.

"Umm, no, Deanna. I don't want you. Go put some clothes on. You're embarrassing yourself. I told you before, Ivy is my girlfriend now."

She didn't move but instead looked around the room. "Well, I don't see her. And here you are, alone in your big bed. I thought you would want some company."

"Well, you thought wrong. And furthermore, Ivy is none of your business. As for you and me, we have a child together—nothing more."

"Oh, Lucas," she went on as if she hadn't heard him. "Don't fight this. We are meant to be together in every way."

He narrowed his eyes at her. "No, we're not. Now get back to the spare room and stay out of here, or you will be back at the hotel tomorrow."

She seemed to get the message this time. Slowly, she got up from the bed and sashayed out of the room in what she most likely thought was a seductive prowl.

Once she was gone, Lucas locked his door, sat down on the side of the bed, and tried to relax. The sight of Deanna naked had repulsed him. What had he ever seen in her? Suddenly, an intense wave of nausea hit him, and he ran into his en suite bathroom and violently threw up. All the contents of his stomach—which was mostly alcohol—came spewing up and into the sink. Then he lay on the cold, marble tile floor and tried to catch his breath. *This situation can't go on. But how am I going to fix it?*

****

Three days after she had gotten the fateful news Lucas had fathered a child with another woman, Ivy was sitting at John F. Kennedy Airport, waiting to board a plane to Boston. Although she had been trying to put the whole situation with Lucas out of her mind, she hadn't been very successful. Nevertheless, she had decided she had cried enough, and after another heartfelt conversation with Jade, it was time to move on.

It was difficult, but she had been through worse. She booted up her laptop to look over her speech but found she couldn't concentrate. Ivy reflected back on the flight she had taken a few months before when a handsome captain had swept her off her feet. Her heart longed for Lucas. But she had to forget everything, for both their sakes.

She hadn't heard from him, and she considered that progress. He probably had his hands full with Deanna and the baby. *Will he get back together with her?* She shuddered at the thought. But from what Ivy had heard about Deanna, she thought maybe Lucas did still have feelings for his former girlfriend. Then she reminded herself that Lucas's love life was really none of her business, not anymore.

Just then, a handsome, young pilot with reddish hair and kind brown eyes came striding toward her. She recognized him at once, as she and Lucas had recently been to their house for dinner with him and his wife, Karen. It had been just a few weeks ago after they got back from Hawaii, but it seemed like a lifetime ago now. Ben McIntyre, Lucas's best friend, was dressed in a crisp white pilot's uniform and smiled as he approached her. Ivy didn't want to be rude, but she didn't want to talk to him either. She would be polite and brief, and then it would be time for her to catch her plane.

"Ivy, hi. May I sit down?" he asked.

Ivy had instantly liked him when she met him, and his wife had been equally kind. But she wasn't sure why he had come over to talk to her since they didn't have anything to talk about now. Despite this fact, she plastered a fake smile on her face. "Hi, Ben. Sure, I've got a few minutes. Have a seat." She gestured to the space beside her and tried to keep her tone light.

"I'm sorry," he said after he sat down. "Y'know, about what happened with you and Lucas."

"Thanks, Ben. Me, too."

"He's devastated that he's lost you, Ivy. I've never seen him like this, and we've been friends forever. In fact, he called in sick today. He never does that."

Ivy's heart sank at the thought of Lucas home alone and sick. Since his family was far away in Florida, he had no one—except Deanna, of course—and that was the problem. And as much as her body ached to go to him, her rational mind reminded her that no matter what she said or did, it wouldn't change the fact Lucas had fathered a child with his ex-girlfriend. He had to take responsibility for that. And there was no longer any room in his life for her.

She smiled in a sad expression. Her fake cheer was long forgotten. "I'm sorry to hear that, but there's nothing I can do. It's a difficult situation for both of us."

"I know, and I hate to meddle. That's usually Karen's job," he joked. "But is there any way you could give him another chance?"

She would have liked nothing better, but it would never work. "I don't think so," she answered. "He's got a big job ahead of him as a father, and I'm afraid I'd just get in the way."

"He doesn't agree with that."

She had hoped he felt that way, and now Ben had just confirmed it. But that didn't mean that, given time, Lucas's feelings for Deanna wouldn't resurface. And then she'd just be back to where she started—alone. It would be less painful in the long run to have ended it all when he had told her the devastating news. She sighed. "I know, but that's the way it is. I'm sorry, Ben. I have to catch my flight now. But when you see Lucas, would you give him a message for me?"

"Absolutely. What is it?"

"Tell him to let go of me. If he doesn't, it's never

going to stop hurting."

And before Ben could respond, she got up and hurried toward her gate. While she waited in line, she couldn't help but silently think to herself, *I should take my own advice.*

****

The next few days were impossible for Lucas. Deanna was more difficult to deal with than he remembered. And although he hadn't found her in his bed again, she was lurking at every turn in his condo, always wanting him to hold the baby, change the baby, and put the baby down for a nap. It was overwhelming, to say the least.

Lucas did all of those things because he wanted to take care of his new son, but he loathed every task. He had wanted to be a father some day, but later in life and with someone he loved—someone like Ivy. And he hadn't been able to go to work and escape her. He had thrown up for two days straight, and while his doctor had labeled it a terrible case of the flu, Lucas knew it was, in fact, a terrible case of a broken heart.

Finally, after four days, he was feeling marginally better, and he needed a break from Deanna and the baby. Little Ryan had been fussing all day, and his constant crying had given Lucas a headache. He had to escape from here. But more importantly, he needed to see Ivy. He wasn't sure if she would see him, but he had to try.

He found Deanna lying on the couch, watching television. The baby was sleeping on the floor beside her.

"I have to go out for a little while."

"Oh, Lucas," she whined. "Why?"

"Ben called," he lied. "He needs my help with something."

"Well, I need your help, too, with little Ryan, and you've been keeping mostly to yourself."

"I told you, Deanna, I had the flu. I didn't want the baby to catch it. But I've been trying to help you the best I can."

She sighed. "I know, but I'm just so lonely when you're not around."

Lucas's stomach churned at her pathetic attempt to entrench him deeper into his life. "I'm sorry," he lied again. "We'll work something out. But right now, I gotta go. Don't wait up. I might be late."

"I'm always waiting, Lucas," she said in a low purr she probably thought was enticing.

Lucas willed himself not to throw up all over her. This conversation was making him feel dreadfully ill, again. But rather than continue this torture, he ignored her comment. "Okay, see you later," he remarked as he bolted for the door.

****

Lucas arrived at Ivy's apartment a half hour later. He had given her back the keys the other day, but the bellman had let him in the front door. After taking the stairs two at a time up to her floor, he knocked on her door. Hoping she was home, he waited.

The door opened a few moments later. A woman stood there, observing him. She had the same violet-blue eyes as Ivy, but her hair was darker and she was quite a bit shorter. *She must be a relative.*

"I'm sorry…"

"You must be Lucas," she stated as she cut him off mid-sentence. Not to mention she was eyeing him with a cold, calculated stare.

"Yes, I was hoping to talk to Ivy," he said, feeling like he was being interrogated.

"She's not here. Ivy went to Boston for a conference. I'm Jade, her sister." She stuck out her hand for him to shake it, and he did. Her touch was cool, firm, and in control. *Geez, Ivy wasn't kidding when she said her sister was a 24/7 cop.*

He had wanted to meet Ivy's sister but not like this. To say she was intimidating was a huge understatement. This couldn't end well. He quickly backed up and started to leave. "Oh well, I apologize for having disturbed you. Would you please tell Ivy I stopped by?"

"Actually, I would like to ask you a few questions, Lucas. Why don't you come inside for a couple of minutes?"

Lucas felt a trepidation he hadn't ever experienced before. He had never been in trouble with the law, and he was no match for this seasoned New York City detective.

Nevertheless, he wasn't in a hurry to get back to Deanna, and he had nothing to hide. He was quite sure Jade knew what had gone on between him and Ivy, and if she wanted to know more, he was an open book. Besides, there was a slim chance he might gain some insight into Ivy's thoughts from her sister. He knew they were close.

"Sure, no problem," he said with a casual tone he didn't feel.

She stepped aside and led him through to the kitchen.

"Would you like some coffee?"

He took off his coat and hung it on the back of the kitchen chair. "Yes, please. Just black." He needed something to hold on to in order to keep his hands from shaking. God, this woman was intense. How did Ivy stand her?

She handed him a cup, and he sat down at the table in Ivy's tiny but cheery kitchen. It was decorated in warm yellow colors with white cupboards. The scenery was in sharp contrast to the icy tone Jade was radiating. Lucas took a deep breath and tried to relax.

Jade grabbed a pen and paper from the counter and sat across from Lucas.

"You don't mind if I take some notes, do you?"

"Am I under investigation?" He had tried to make a joke, but her look said she wasn't amused.

"No. But I'm going to be honest with you, Lucas. I've been a police officer for a very long time, and there is something about this whole situation with your ex-girlfriend. She still is your ex, isn't she?"

"Yes, very much so."

"Good. Anyway, something about this doesn't sit right with me. And although I promised Ivy I wouldn't get involved, here you are, and we are just going to have a nice friendly conversation. Sound good?"

"Umm, I guess. What do you want to know?"

She shook her head at him. "No guessing, Lucas. Yes or no. I need you to be upfront and honest. No games. And I'll return the same courtesy to you."

Lucas was stunned with her bold tone, but he was intrigued as to what she thought. "Yes, go ahead. Ask me anything." And she did.

An hour later, she had asked him every question possible about Deanna, the baby, the timing, and even the lab that did the paternity test. Lucas had even told her he suspected Deanna of cheating on him when they were together, although he had no concrete proof of that. And he had completely dismissed that fact once he got the results of the paternity test. But nevertheless, he had mentioned it. He was exhausted by her attention to detail, and she took meticulous notes. She would strike fear in the heart of any criminal; that was for sure.

But he could also tell she was good at her job and was looking out for her baby sister. There was no way he could fault her for that. When she seemed to be wrapping up her interrogation, he couldn't help but ask the question that had been bouncing around in his head during their entire conversation. "Jade, please tell me. What do you think is going on?"

She pursed her lips. "Well, I can't say for sure, but it's definitely worth looking into. I will let you know if I find anything out."

He nodded. "Thank you. But it seems pretty cut-and-dried to me. I messed up and got my crazy former girlfriend pregnant."

She frowned at him. "Why don't you leave the detective work to me, okay?"

"Okay," he agreed.

"I'll be in touch."

Lucas stood to leave, and he shook her hand again. This time, however, he sensed she had thawed ever so slightly toward him. They reached the front door, and she turned to him again.

"Lucas," she said with unexpected emotion in her voice. "I don't know exactly what you've gotten yourself into, but I promise you, if Deanna is hiding anything, I'm going to find out about it. Ivy still loves you. You were the one who brought her back to life after—well, you know. So I'm not going to let this go until I get some answers. It may take a bit of digging, but I will find out what happened."

Lucas sighed. "I love her, too. I just wish things were different. Can't you convince her to give me another chance?"

Jade shook her head. "Believe it or not, Ivy is more stubborn than me. There's no convincing her of anything. She thinks you belong with your son and his mother. So I just want to make sure that is what's happening here. Good night, Lucas."

"Good night, Jade."

And with his head swimming with insane possibilities, he made his way back to his condo and Deanna.

****

Ivy made it to Boston and back without too many complications. It wasn't her most stellar seminar, but she did the best she could. Jade was waiting for her at her apartment when she arrived back early one afternoon.

"Hey, big sister," she said when she opened her apartment door and Jade was standing there. The two women embraced in a warm hug.

"What are you doing here? Shouldn't you be out solving crimes?"

"Funny, but no," Jade replied. "I do get a few days off here and there, you know."

Ivy rolled her eyes at her sister. "Whatever. You haven't taken a day off in as long as I can remember."

"Well, I did today. I knew you were coming back, and I wanted to be here to check on you. How did it go in Boston?"

Ivy smiled. "Thank you, but I'm good, really. The conference went well; I'm getting my groove back. My agent will be most impressed."

Jade returned the gesture. "That's great. Well, drop your bags, and then we'll go for a walk and get some lunch."

"Oh, Jade, I don't know. I'm tired."

Jade frowned. "No excuses. If you are truly as fine as you want me to believe, you'll go out. I'm not going to let you doze on the couch watching trash television for the entire weekend."

Why does she always see right through me? "Okay, just give me a minute to put my stuff away."

"Sure," Jade said. "Take your time, but don't put your pajamas on."

"Oh, my sister the comic. Stick to your day job."

"Trust me, I am."

Ivy smiled and wandered into the bedroom to drop off her bags. She called back over her shoulder to Jade. "Did you water the plants? Did I miss any excitement here?"

"Yes, I watered the plants. Oh, and Lucas stopped by to see you."

"What?" Ivy exclaimed and ran back out to the living room to face her sister.

"Did you talk to him? What did he say?"

"He wanted to see you. I invited him in for a chat."

Ivy groaned. "Jade, no…"

"Oh, relax. I was perfectly pleasant. He still loves you. Lucas wants you back, Ivy."

At the mention of his name, her skin flushed with heat and desire. She remembered the last time he was here with her and the mad, passionate night of ecstasy they had shared. And as usual, no matter how hard she tried to hide it, Jade noticed everything.

"Hmm," Jade said thoughtfully. "It's exactly what I suspected. You still love him, too."

"No, I—"

"Don't try and deny it, little sister. It's written all over your face. You don't need to be a trained investigator to see that. But nevertheless, I am, so you can't get anything by me."

Ivy sat down on her sofa and put her head in her hands. After a few moments of silence, she looked up at Jade. "Okay. Yes, I still love him. But so what? It's never going to work. He has a child with another woman—one he used to date. He needs to concentrate on that."

Jade pursed her lips. "Well, that remains to be seen."

"What does that mean?" Ivy asked.

"Never mind. Put your coat on, and let's go eat some junk food."

Ivy was too weary to argue, so she just did as she was told. It was an old and familiar pattern where her big sister was concerned. She never got information out of Jade that she didn't want to share. Furthermore, she hadn't won an argument with her—ever—and she knew she never would.

****

Lucas spent the next week throwing himself back into his work. Taking extra shifts when he could, he was flying almost all the time. It was like old times, before Ivy. Boring and very depressing.

But not nearly as bad as spending time with

Deanna and the baby. She wasn't budging on getting her own place, as she had taken over his condo with her stuff laying around everywhere. It was a mess. Not to mention, she let the baby cry, almost non-stop. Not the stellar mother figure she tried to convince him she was when she showed up on his doorstep. When he was home, he looked after little Ryan as best he could, but his heart just wasn't in it.

And Deanna had developed a nasty habit of taking off when Lucas was home with the baby. She left for hours on end, never saying where she had been or what she had been doing. Lucas had switched the baby to formula, since Deanna was unreliable and had been drinking again—and probably more than that—on many occasions.

Karen had been over quite a bit to help Lucas out. He was lost when it came to infants, but Karen was a natural mother. She showed Lucas how to bathe and feed little Ryan and held him for hours while Lucas slept after working eighteen-hour shifts. Lucas was just sorry Ben and Karen hadn't been able to have a baby of their own. Life could be so cruel sometimes.

But if Lucas wasn't working and Deanna was home, he spent most nights at Ben and Karen's apartment. He just couldn't bring himself to go home. And besides, with Deanna and the baby there, it didn't feel like his place anymore anyway.

Ben said he and Karen didn't mind, but Lucas couldn't let this go on much longer. He hadn't heard from Jade, so he just assumed the story was exactly how he told her. And despite his constant texts and messages to Ivy, she hadn't responded to any of them. Lucas had made the biggest mistake of his life, and now he was paying the ultimate price.

One late morning, he was just folding up the blankets on the bed in the spare room when Ben walked in, holding out Lucas's cellphone to him. He had purposely left it on the table by the front door when he and Ben had arrived back from a round-trip flight at four o'clock this morning. If he hadn't, Deanna would have kept him up all night with her constant texts and calls.

"Sorry man," Ben whispered, handing it to him. "But she just won't stop."

"I know," he said, accepting the phone from Ben's outstretched hand. He was wishing he had dropped it out of the plane at thirty-five thousand feet last night when he was flying.

"Hello," he said into the phone, a deadpan tone to his voice.

"Lucas, thank goodness you finally answered. I've been calling and texting. Where have you been?"

He sighed. "I told you, Deanna, I'm working. I just got back from Washington."

"Well, when are you coming home?" she whined into the phone. "Ryan and I miss you, and we've been stuck here waiting."

"You don't have to wait for me. You can go out with the baby on your own, you know."

"But it's not fun without you. Are you going to take us out today?"

Lucas looked out the window and saw the beautiful winter sun shining.

"Sure. Why don't you meet me at Central Park in an hour, over by the pond? I'm sure the baby would like the fresh air."

"Okay," she said. "But then will you at least take us to dinner at a nice restaurant?"

"That sounds great," he lied. "See you in a little while."

He disconnected and then saw Ben standing a few feet away from him with a sympathetic look on his face. "Do I want to know?" he asked.

"No," he replied. "You don't."

Chapter Nine

Ivy and Jade were walking in Central Park, laughing and enjoying the rare warm winter day. The sun was shining, and they were just making their way over to the hot dog stand to get some lunch. Jade was telling Ivy some tales about the recent arrests she had made. It was like an episode of the world's worst criminal, and Ivy was laughing so hard her stomach was hurting.

They were just rounding the pond when Ivy saw a striking figure waiting just off to the side of the path. She would have recognized his tall, muscular form from a mile away. It was Lucas. He looked tired—worn out really—and she watched as he ran his hands through his golden-streaked hair. It was getting longer and looked somewhat unkempt. Dark shades hid his eyes, and he was in desperate need of a shave. But he was still unbelievably handsome. Dressed in khaki cargo pants and a black bomber jacket, he appeared to be waiting for someone.

She stopped dead in her tracks and almost tripped over Jade.

"What the..." Jade started to say and then stopped as she followed Ivy's gaze. "Oh, it's him. Ivy, go over and say something."

"No, I can't," Ivy replied in a whisper. "Besides, he hasn't seen me. Let's just leave."

"C'mon, little sister. Stop denying your true feelings. Go say hi to him now, or I will."

"You wouldn't."

Jade smiled. "Are you daring me?"

Ivy shook her head. "No, I learned that lesson the hard way."

"Good. I'll go get our lunch. Meet me at the hot dog stand—or don't. It's up to you. Either way, text me."

"Jade…" Ivy pleaded.

But she was already walking away, leaving Ivy standing all alone.

Ivy took a deep breath and made her way over to the love of her life. He looked uncomfortable, which was very unusual for him. She continued to stare at him, but he appeared not to notice anything or anyone around him. Finally taking pity on him, she walked right over to where he was standing.

"Hey, Lucas," she said, trying to catch his eye, although she couldn't see through his dark sunglasses. He looked over at her, taking them off. His eyes were shadowed, showing extreme fatigue—or was it depression? She couldn't tell for sure.

"Ivy, hi," he replied, focusing on her. He smiled a sad smile, and Ivy almost melted on the spot. She wanted to throw herself into his arms and erase all the pain. Instead, she steadied herself and continued to gaze at his pained expression.

He finally broke the silence. "I guess everyone's out for a walk on this beautiful day, eh?"

So this was it. They were reduced to small talk, like acquaintances or old friends. So be it.

"Yes," she replied with a fake cheeriness. "I was

just going to have lunch with Jade when I saw you." Then she couldn't stand this anymore and heard herself blurting out, "Lucas, is everything all right?"

"No, it's not," he said, his voice full of unexpected tenderness. "Ivy, I'm falling apart without you. Can't you see that?"

Her eyes filled with tears at his blunt statement. She, too, was falling apart. But apparently, she was better at hiding it, for the most part.

"Oh, Lucas," she whispered. She didn't know what else to say to him, so instead, she walked over and put her arms around him.

He enveloped her, and she clung to him. His embrace was so inviting and familiar. Nothing had changed, and everything had changed. He smelled of his signature white musk scent, and she inhaled deeply. *I miss him. I miss this.*

He leaned down and kissed her temple. The contact of his lips on her skin had her heart racing. Then he whispered in her ear. "I can't do this anymore. Being away from you is killing me."

She was about to reply she felt the same when she heard a shrill, familiar voice. "Well, isn't this cozy."

They both turned to see Deanna standing there in a tight leather jacket, short skirt, and heels. *Not exactly the appropriate attire for a walk in Central Park.* She had the baby bundled in a stroller and a murderous look on her face. Ivy tried to back away from Lucas, but he held her tight. Seeing this further infuriated Deanna. "What's the matter, Ivy? Can't find your own man, so you're trying to steal mine?"

"Deanna, stop," Lucas said.

"What, Lucas? Didn't you tell her we are living

together now?"

Ivy backed away, out of his arms. "Is that true?" Shock and disbelief were no doubt etched on her face.

"It's a temporary situation," he said tightly.

Deanna rolled her eyes. "Oh, Lucas, don't try to spare her feelings. She knows we are a family now, don't you, Ivy?"

Ivy ignored Deanna and gazed at Lucas. He looked away, unable to meet her eyes. That was proof enough for her.

She turned her back on the two of them and walked away from Lucas Freeman for what she promised herself was the last time.

****

The next few days were hell for Lucas. After the incident at Central Park, he knew he had lost Ivy forever. Deanna was more than thrilled and was still trying to worm her way into every aspect of his life. Thank goodness for work and Ben. They were the only things that were keeping him sane right now.

One afternoon, Lucas was just home from a cross-country flight. He should get some sleep, but since Deanna had taken the baby out to meet some friends, he took the opportunity to clean up his condo. Deanna was a slob and never cooked or did housework. Food, dirty diapers, and soiled clothing were everywhere. She never picked up after herself or the baby. He had started to look for a studio apartment he could rent. It was clear she wasn't leaving, so he had decided to just give her the condo and move out. Unfortunately, studios were somewhat difficult to come by, but he had a realtor working hard on finding him one.

The doorbell rang and Lucas sighed. Was Deanna

back already? He had half a mind to just go to his room and crash, but she would find him. So he went to let her in, even though she had her own key now.

He opened the door to find Jade standing there, looking as intense as usual. She was dressed in a smart navy pantsuit, and her dark-blonde hair was pulled back into a tight bun. He could see the slight bulge by her hip, indicating she was carrying a firearm. She wasn't afraid to use it, and the way he had been feeling lately, he wasn't sure he cared if she did. Lucas knew Jade loved Ivy deeply. What he wasn't sure of was what she would do to the man who had broken her sister's heart.

"Jade," he said, trying to hide his surprise and recover some semblance of composure. She was probably here to tear his head off. Best to just apologize. "I'm sorry about what happened—"

She cut him off. "Let's not worry about that right now. I need to speak with you. Is Deanna here?"

"No, she's out."

"Good. May I come in?"

"Of course," he said, remembering his manners. "Please come inside."

She followed him in, and he took her coat. He led her through the disastrous living room and into the kitchen. It was the least messy part of this whole place since Deanna never cooked and was rarely in here.

"Can I get you a drink?" he asked as he gestured for her to sit at the table.

"No, I'm fine. Thanks. But you may need one after I tell you what I found out."

"What?" he said, confused and taken aback. *Maybe she isn't here to kill me.*

"Just listen," she said in a clipped tone, and he

leaned in toward her so he wouldn't miss a word.

She pulled a file out of her briefcase and opened it up.

She sighed and looked him in the eye. "You are not going to believe what Deanna Mason has been up to. Everything she has told you is a lie."

"What do you mean?" He had hoped this was true, but he still didn't think it was possible.

"Let's start from the beginning. Near the end of your relationship, you were right. She was seeing someone else—one Rene Sinclair to be exact. He was a lowlife drug dealer whom the narcotics officers at the division were more than happy to tell me all about. In fact, he and Deanna got arrested for possession of heroin. I came across this information when I ran her name through the system. Unfortunately, they couldn't make the charges stick to her. She claimed she was just the innocent girlfriend, carrying his child. It was right there in the police report. Then, at the time you mentioned she just took off on you, Rene got out on bail. They fled to New Jersey, not Kentucky as she told you. He was wanted on a warrant for breaching his bail conditions, and sometime when they were on the run, she gave birth to Ryan Sinclair. Did you ever see the baby's birth certificate, Lucas?"

"No," he said, his confusion turning to anger. Could this be true? It had to be. Jade wasn't the lying type, but Deanna sure was.

"Well, I did and look here. It says Ryan Sinclair, not Ryan Mason as Deanna told you." She handed him a copy of the paperwork, and he studied it. She was indeed correct.

"But what about—"

"I'll get to that. Just listen."

"Anyway, the baby had just turned three months when Daddy Sinclair gets caught up in a drug deal gone bad. Two rounds in the chest from a forty-five caliber had him hanging out at the morgue, not the nursery. So now, little Ryan is fatherless and Deanna is penniless. So who does she think of? You."

"But—"

"Lucas, do you know what I do to suspects who keep interrupting me? Well, you don't want to find out, so shut up."

He fell silent, but his head was trying to process what Jade was saying. *What the hell?*

"Now she's thought of you, looked you up, and you're still living in New York. She knows you're rich and hopes you're still single. But how is she going to convince you to take her back? Well, as charming as she is, she knows that might not work. So she decides to pass off the baby as yours. After all, you have the same complexion and eye color as Rene, so it's a possibility, right?" She paused.

"Right," he said, although he had no idea this was the case. *Where is this going?*

"Anyway, she knows you are smart and would insist on a paternity test. So this is a problem. Well, it would be for most people, but not for a woman like Deanna who has connections in the world of criminal enterprise. So she finds a lab that will—for a price, of course—give you the paternity test results you request, and not necessarily the accurate ones. I've looked into this lab, and they have many complaints against them, everything from false test results to misplaced samples. I'm a bit surprised they haven't been shut down yet, but

I'm working on that." She paused and eyed him with what he thought looked like a sympathetic expression. "I know this is a lot to take in, but you do have a lot of work to do and some serious decisions to make."

Lucas's head was spinning. He got up and reached for a bottle of whiskey in the cupboard. He pulled out two glasses and brought them to the table. "Are you sure you don't want one?"

"Oh, why not," she said. "I'm off the clock, and you have great taste in whiskey. Pour me a glass."

He got out the ice cubes, added the strong alcohol to the tumblers, and sat back down.

She took a sip of the amber liquid. "Wow," she said. "That's good."

Lucas downed his shot in a matter of seconds and poured himself another.

"Okay," Jade said, all businesslike again. She removed the bottle from his grasp. "That's enough of that. We're not done here."

"Oh, I'm done," Lucas said, finding his voice again. "I can't handle any more. That bitch has ruined my life, and I was so stupid to buy her entire story without asking a single intelligent question. I have no idea where to go from here."

"Lucas," Jade said harshly. "Man up. Deanna is to blame for this whole situation. You couldn't have known—not without my connections. And mark my words, we will make her pay. Now it's time to take action and reclaim your life."

"What life? I've lost Ivy forever. She made it pretty clear it's over between us. Besides, once she hears how I believed all of Deanna's lies, she'll never want me back, and I can't say I blame her."

"Hey, what are you saying? Never mind, you're talking crazy. Once we get this whole mess sorted out, I'm ordering you to go to her. Tell her everything. She will take you back. She still loves you, Lucas; I know it. Now, I'm going to help you with your next steps."

Next steps? I can't handle this.

"You have to bring the baby for a new paternity test at the NYPD forensics lab tomorrow morning. I guarantee you are not the father, but we need concrete proof. In the meantime, don't say anything to Deanna. Once we have the results, we can have her arrested for falsifying tests or extortion. It's up to you if you want to press charges, but regardless, we don't want her getting a heads-up and bolting. So keep quiet—for now. I'll let you think about it, and we can talk more tomorrow when you come in for the test. I'll meet you there. It only takes an hour for the results, so we can talk while we wait."

Lucas looked at Jade and almost told her to forget the whole thing. But he couldn't let her down; she had done so much for him. He would do whatever she asked, because if there were any chance he could get Ivy back, he had to try.

"Okay, sure. That sounds fine. I'll see you tomorrow then. And Jade, thanks. I can't believe you did all this for me."

"For you and Ivy, Lucas. You deserve to be happy, and I'm not going to let this lying criminal stand in your way."

She got up and handed him back the bottle. "Have another drink, but don't overdo it. You have an important appointment in the morning, and your future sister-in-law will kick your ass if you don't show up."

Lucas smiled at her comment and got up to walk her to the door. When she had gotten her coat on, she turned to Lucas. Quite unexpectedly, she embraced him. "You're a good man, Lucas Freeman, and my sister needs you. So let's make this happen."

He nodded at her and with a confidence he was suddenly beginning to feel said, "Yes, I promise you, I will."

****

A few days later, everything was falling into place. All Lucas had to do now was throw Deanna out. He had debated about what to do with regard to pressing charges but had decided against it. In the end, he just wanted this whole mess over with. He had packed up her belongings while she was out for the morning and put them in a waiting taxi downstairs. When she walked through his front door, it would be for the last time.

Lucas felt a little guilty about what would happen with the baby. But he realized he couldn't raise someone else's child with a woman he didn't love. He had made some arrangements he hoped Deanna would accept, and that was the best he could do.

Her key turned in the lock, and he steeled himself to be strong.

Deanna walked in with the baby on her hip and saw him sitting on the couch. He could barely stand the sight of her since he had discovered what she had done. But getting angry would only make this scene that much worse, so he took a deep breath instead.

"Lucas," she cooed when she saw him. "I'm so glad you're here. I thought you'd be out with Ben or working."

"No, Deanna. We need to talk. Why don't you sit

down?"

She didn't really argue with him, as he thought she might. She seemed to sense something was wrong.

"Okay," she said. "Is everything all right?"

"No, not really."

She sat down next to him and tried to grasp his hand. He pulled away from her and stood up. There was no easy way to say what he had to say, so he just blurted it out.

"I know Ryan is not my son. You falsified the paternity test and tried to pass him off as mine."

Her eyes went wide. "Lucas, no. What on earth made you think that?"

"A New York City detective, who's a friend, looked into the situation for me. Here's the birth certificate and the paternity test from the NYPD forensics lab."

He handed her copies of the paperwork, but she didn't take it.

"Lucas," she said in her syrupy, sweet voice, "of course Ryan is yours. Look at him."

She held the baby out to him, but he backed away. His anger got a hold of him then and he shouted. "Stop lying, Deanna, and admit it. I can have you arrested for this."

The baby started to fuss and Lucas groaned. Then he took a deep breath to calm himself down as he waited to see what she was going to say.

"Okay, okay," she said. "It's true; you're not the biological father. But you don't understand, Lucas. He could be your son. We can still be a family. I'm sorry I lied but—"

"I don't want to hear your excuses. But here is

what I do want, you out of my house and life—now. I've booked you a plane ticket to anywhere you want to go. You can pick it up at the airport. A taxi with all of your things in it is waiting for you downstairs."

She was crying openly now, but he was pretty sure it was just a pathetic ploy to get him to change his mind. "Lucas, what about little Ryan? He doesn't have a father—"

He cut her off. "No, Deanna, he doesn't. But you can't make a father out of someone who isn't. It's not fair to everyone involved."

Taking another deep breath, he told her the last part of her plan. "Deanna, look," he said. "I'm not Ryan's father, and even though you are his birth mother, I'm not sure you have it in you to raise him by yourself."

"I don't, Lucas. That's why I need you."

"Well, that's not going to happen, so I'm going to make a suggestion here. I think you should give Ryan up for adoption. I know a great lawyer who can take him for you right now and place him with a wonderful family. Here's his card." He handed her the piece of paper, and she studied it.

"All you have to do is take Ryan to his office. He will handle everything from there. I can't make you do this, Deanna, but I think Ryan deserves to be in a home with two loving parents, and that's not us."

She stared at him for a long moment and didn't say anything.

He continued. "Whether or not you do this is up to you. But for once in your life, I'm begging you, think about someone other than yourself and make the right decision."

She finally spoke, but it wasn't what he wanted to

hear.

"Lucas, please don't do this. I love you—"

"Enough, Deanna. You don't love me; you never did. And the feeling is mutual. All you did was use me, and I almost fell for it. But thankfully, I've discovered your lies. We have nothing more to say to each other, so it's time for you to leave."

He got up and walked toward the front door. She followed behind him with the baby in her arms, clearly not ready to give up the life she had created for herself—one built on lies and without a single thought as to how it would affect Lucas.

"Whatever decision you make, let's be clear on one thing, I never want to see or hear from you again, or I will press charges against you."

"Lucas," she pleaded again, but he ignored her. She reached for him, but he quickly moved out of her grasp.

"Don't touch me." He flung his front door open. "Goodbye, Deanna."

Lucas shut the door in her shocked face and collapsed to the floor, exhausted from the heated exchange. He could still hear her on the other side, imploring him to open up the door. Getting up, he made his way into the living room so he didn't have to listen to her anymore. He walked around, cleaning up the mess she had left in her wake. And as he did, he began to feel something he hadn't felt in quite some time— hope.

Chapter Ten

A week after Ivy had seen Lucas in Central Park, she was desperately trying to get on with her life. Her worst fear had come true, Lucas was living with the mother of his child and it was over between them. In the end, she had been the one to push him away, but nevertheless, her pain was not diminished by that fact.

Ivy had almost canceled her upcoming seminar in Toronto; she didn't know how she would get through it. But Jade had been by several times to her apartment, and she was trying to put on a brave face for her sister. She figured Jade could see right through her, but it wasn't for lack of trying.

So instead of bailing out on the organizers of the conference, she decided to go to Toronto a few days before she was scheduled to present. Ivy thought she might visit some of the sights of that beautiful city, and a change of scenery was definitely in order. Jade had heartily encouraged her to take the earlier flight, so Ivy did as she was told to by her big sister—again.

Besides, everywhere she went in New York reminded her of Lucas: the restaurants and cafes they had visited, the museums and, of course, Central Park. All had memories of happy times with Lucas, and she couldn't bear them. Not right now. Ivy needed a break from all of it. Toronto was fresh and new, and she'd always loved going there. It was one of the few places she had always gone alone, so no ghosts lurked in that city.

Late one afternoon, she was sitting on the plane at John F. Kennedy Airport in New York, waiting to take off for Toronto. She watched as the last of the passengers boarded and thought about getting her speech out to practice it. Resilience was her new topic of interest, and she felt she had not only researched it but had also lived it for the past few months. Then she decided against working and thought she'd take a nap instead. She was tired, and she could always look at her tablet later. Leaning back in her seat, she closed her eyes and tried to relax.

Flying had gotten easier for her now that she was traveling with regularity again. Despite the hustle and bustle of people going by her section, Ivy found herself beginning to drift off.

Just then, the speaker overhead came on, and she couldn't believe what she was hearing. The smooth, sexy voice that she had heard in her sleep every night for as long as they had been apart, began to speak.

"Good afternoon, ladies and gentlemen," Lucas began in the deep baritone which had mesmerized her three months earlier on a flight just like this one.

Ivy's eyes flew open in surprise. Was it too late to exit the plane? She glanced at the entrance. Yes, they had already closed the doors. Did he know she was on board? It was impossible to be certain.

Having no other viable option, she listened to the sound of her former lover as he continued to speak.

"I'm Captain Lucas Freeman, and my co-pilot is Ben McIntyre. On behalf of myself and the flight crew, we would like to welcome you aboard Fantasy Flight

9478 which is non-stop to Pearson International Airport in Toronto. Our flying time is one hour and twenty-five minutes. The skies look clear for this short trip. The weather is an unseasonably warm fifty-five degrees Fahrenheit in Toronto. I hope you enjoy your flight."

God, she wanted him. Ivy had to restrain herself from leaping up out of her seat and running to the cockpit door. It was over. She had to accept that. Besides, she reasoned, he'd probably switched from his cross-country flights to these shorter hauls in order to spend more time with Deanna and the baby.

But the more she told herself she didn't want him, the more she did. Eventually, she decided to just keep quiet in her seat and pray he didn't have time to read the passenger manifest. Then another painful, awkward situation could be avoided. Yes, that would be the best course of action.

She slouched down and listened, despite herself.

"We are just about to get ready to exit the gate and take our place in line for takeoff. But before we do, I'd like to mention an extraordinary passenger whom we have onboard today."

Oh no. Were Deanna and the baby on the plane? Ivy looked around but didn't see them in the first-class section. He continued before Ivy could panic too much.

"My girlfriend, Ivy, is sitting in seat 3-B today. We've been through a lot of turbulence to get to where we are today. But I'm here to tell you, our problems have gone away—for good. I love you with all my heart and soul. The day I met you was the day my life truly became worth living, and I want to spend every second from this moment on with you. Ivy, will you please do me the honor of marrying me?"

Tears welled in Ivy's eyes, and Lucas appeared by her side. He was as handsome as ever in his crisp, white uniform. His hair was cut, and he had shaved his goatee. His emerald eyes were shining with unshed tears, and in his hand was a small turquoise box. He knelt down in front of her and opened it.

Ivy was overcome with emotion and rendered speechless. But she managed to gasp when he opened the box, revealing a brilliant stunning pavé engagement ring. It had a large, round diamond in the center and was encircled on either side with smaller ones. The white gold band was encrusted with tiny, sparkling gems.

"Oh, Lucas," Ivy said, finally finding her voice.

"Ivy, I'm so sorry about everything we've been through. It turns out Deanna was lying the entire time. The baby wasn't mine. But she's gone, Ivy, for good this time. Can you find it in your heart to forgive me for this terrible ordeal?"

"What?" Ivy said. So much was happening at once.

"I'll explain everything later, I promise. Meet me at the Royal Hotel when we land. I reserved a suite for us under my name. But in the meantime, everyone is watching us to hear whether or not you will become my wife."

Ivy looked around, and indeed, everyone in first class was watching them with bated breath. Her head was spinning with the words he had just spoken. But she didn't have to think about her response to his question. She knew the answer was in her heart—ever since Lucas had stolen it just a few short months ago.

"Yes, Lucas," she said loudly so the other passengers could hear. "It would be my great privilege to marry you."

The words had barely left her mouth when he swept her up out of her seat and into his embrace. Their lips met in a blaze of passion. The small crowd cheered, but all of Ivy's senses were focused on Lucas. They kissed long and deep, and she realized how much she had missed this when they were apart. She craved him. His hands cupped the back of her neck, and she tasted peppermint on his breath. She ran her hands through his hair. It was so warm and comforting to be in his arms again.

After a few moments, he broke it off. He slipped the beautiful ring on her finger, and it was a perfect fit.

"Lucas, it's gorgeous, but—"

"No buts. It's a nice ring but not half as gorgeous as you are. And if you are going to be my wife, you're keeping it."

"Okay," she said, smiling. "Thank you; I love it."

"And I love you. And I hate to cut this short, but I have to go fly the plane now, or the passengers will start complaining."

She laughed. "I know. Your antics have probably delayed everything."

"It was worth it."

"Go," she admonished. "I'll see you in Toronto."

He kissed her again, softly this time, and then he was off.

Ivy leaned back in her seat. Wow. She could hardly believe what had just happened. She still had lots of questions, of course. But one thing was for sure, this day had turned out more unbelievably perfect than any other she could have ever imagined.

****

Lucas couldn't wipe the grin off his face as he made his way back to the cockpit. Ben was waiting for him with a smile on his face almost as big as Lucas's.

"So what did she say?" Ben asked. "Because I can't really tell from the look on your face."

Lucas grabbed him in a big hug and let out a huge breath he didn't know he had been holding. "She said yes, man. I still can't believe it."

"C'mon. What woman in her right mind would turn down that huge diamond ring you bribed her with?"

Lucas just laughed. He was so happy, he didn't think anything anyone said could ruin this mood.

"Just joking, you know that."

"I know," Lucas said and smiled at his best friend.

"You're a pretty great guy, and Ivy is a wonderful woman. You both deserve to be happy, especially after everything you've been through. But you know what this means, don't you?"

"No, what's that?" Lucas asked.

"Karen is going to want to throw you a huge engagement party, and she won't take no for an answer."

Lucas grinned again. "I'm sure Ivy would love that. Besides, I owe Karen big time for practically living in your spare room for the last month."

The two men laughed, and then Ben slapped him on the shoulder.

"Oh, and one more thing," Ben said.

Lucas groaned, thinking Ben was about to crack another one of his bad jokes.

"No, I'm serious," he said. "I just got off the phone with Karen. Our adoption lawyer just called. They have a baby for us. Karen is ecstatic. I've never heard her more excited about anything. It's a three-month-old boy named Ryan. Lucas, you did this, didn't you? You made our dream come true."

Lucas let out a long sigh. Deanna had actually done what he had asked, and he was astounded. It was a miracle on so many levels. He hadn't wanted to mention it to Ben—just in case things didn't pan out—but he was so glad they had.

Lucas paused for a moment before he spoke to Ben. "Well, I set it up, but I honestly didn't know if she would go through with it. I'm so happy she did. You and Karen are going to be wonderful parents. Ben, you're my dearest friend, so I just had to try and convince her. It was the best possible scenario, for everyone's sake. I'm so glad it worked out."

Ben now had tears in his eyes, and he grabbed Lucas in a fierce embrace.

"I love you, man. And I don't know how to ever thank you," Ben said.

"No thanks needed," Lucas replied, tearing up himself. "I know you and Karen will raise Ryan with all the love he deserves, and that's more than enough for me."

"We will, Lucas, I promise you."

After a minute, Ben recovered his composure and said to Lucas, "Okay, Captain, that's enough crying for one day. I guess we should get back to work."

"Yes. Time for takeoff."

****

Once they landed in Toronto, Ivy went through customs and collected her bags. Then, she stepped into a quiet area off the terminal to phone Jade. She couldn't wait to tell her what had happened. Usually, she got her voicemail, but strangely, this time her sister picked up the call.

"Hi, Ivy," she said brightly. "Everything okay in Toronto?"

"Hi, Jade. Yes, I—"

"Did you see him? Did he ask you? Do you have that knockout ring on your finger?"

Ivy was stunned into silence. When she finally found her voice, she said, "How did you—"

"Lucas told me everything. Don't be mad, Ivy, but after Lucas came to your apartment a few weeks ago, we talked, and I started looking into things. Turns out, Deanna was lying—about everything. I helped Lucas sort it out and then…well, he can tell you the whole story. But let me say this. After he got rid of her, he wanted to surprise you. Did he?"

"Yes!" Ivy exclaimed. "I was so surprised I couldn't speak. I can't believe you did all this, Jade, but I'm so glad. And I'm so lucky to have a sister like you. Thank you."

"No need for thanks, little sister. That devious witch got what was coming to her. I was just relieved I could figure out the truth for both of you. And she's out of the picture. Now I think you have a date with a handsome captain. Am I wrong?"

"No, you're right, as usual."

"Good. Well, get going. We will catch up when you get home."

"Okay, love you. Bye."

"Bye. Love you, too. Give Lucas a hug for me," Jade said.

They hung up, and Ivy stared at the phone in awe. Jade and Lucas doing all of this for her? She sure was one lucky woman, and she wasn't going to forget it—ever. And with that thought in mind, she raced off to meet her new fiancé.

****

Lucas was pacing around the room at the hotel, waiting for Ivy. He had reserved the most luxurious suite they had to offer on the sixteenth floor. The large space boasted a beautiful, king-size bed done in soft coral hues, and there was a spacious sitting area with a sofa and two chairs. The furniture was done in a complementary ivory color with a hint of Victorian flair. Stunning views of the city could be seen from that height.

Room service had been by to drop off a bottle of champagne and an elegant sushi platter with various kinds of the delicacy. Chocolate covered strawberries completed the meal. Lucas had insisted on them since he knew they were Ivy's favorite. They had set it all up on the elegant glass table.

Lucas had just showered and changed out of his uniform. He was dressed in dark jeans and a soft, plaid shirt. He wasn't sure what she would want to do tonight, but he hoped to keep the mood light. And as well as the very public proposal had gone, the only person he wanted to see for the next two days was Ivy. He hoped she felt the same. His body and soul were aching to have her back.

Wanting to calm his nerves, he selected a single malt scotch from the minibar and poured himself a glass. The smooth, gold liquid tasted of vanilla with a hint of smoke. But more importantly, it calmed down the tension he was feeling.

He knew he and Ivy were back together, but he just

had to see her and talk to her alone before this unease would completely disappear. He also needed to hold her—all night. His heart had been heavy every time he went to bed alone. Thank goodness those days were over.

A sharp knock at the door roused him from his thoughts. He rushed to open it. Ivy was standing there, looking gorgeous in a short wool coat and pink scarf. She was dressed in jeans as well and had a small suitcase with her. Her hair was pulled back into an elegant twist, and she smiled at him.

"Hi," she whispered.

"Hi," he replied and pulled her into his arms.

The door shut behind them, and he wrapped her in a tight embrace. He inhaled her intoxicating rose scent, and she melted into him. Leaning down, he kissed her, softly at first and then with more emotion. Their tongues entwined, and he tasted the raspberry gum she always loved to chew.

He reached up and pulled the pins from her hair. Her long, white-blonde waves cascaded down her back, and he softly touched the delicate locks. She reached her arms around his neck and pulled him even closer. He could feel his arousal for her growing. He wanted her—now.

But no, this wasn't fair to Ivy. She needed to hear the whole story and then he could make mad, passionate love to her all night long.

"Ivy," he breathed, barely holding himself together. "We should talk."

"Later," she said with desire in her voice. "Right now, I just want you to undress me."

"But," he said again, trying to be the gentleman she

wanted. "Don't you want to know about—"

"No." Reaching for the buttons on his shirt, she tore them open.

He shrugged the shirt off and tossed it to the floor.

She kissed his chest, and he groaned with need. He leaned on the wall for support as she worked her way down to his belt buckle.

Then she looked up at him with her stunning violet-blue eyes and said, "Still want to talk, Lucas?"

"Later," he ground out, and he reached for the tie on her coat. He helped her out of it, then threw it aside and removed her scarf. She was wearing a blue shirt underneath, and he peeled that off of her, revealing a red, satin push-up bra. He sighed at the gorgeous sight in front of him and pressed her bare flesh against his. She responded to the contact with a moan of her own.

He picked her up and carried her over to the bed. He gently set her down on the silk duvet. Sitting down beside her, he reached for the waistband of her jeans and slid his hand inside. She arched up to meet him and breathed out his name. Lucas was almost undone at the sight of her like this—so sexual and full of need—need he would fulfill for her, now and forever. He moved his fingers inside of her and she came, calling out his name.

He was on the edge and quickly removed his jeans and hers. She was still quivering as they lay naked beside each other. He turned her over on her stomach, massaging her back and planting kisses on the back of her neck. She moaned with pleasure, and he climbed on top of her. Hanging on by a thread, he pulled her hips up to meet him and drove into her from behind. He was instantly enveloped by her slick warmth. He began to thrust, and she groaned her approval beneath him. But the buildup had been so intense, he came, roaring her name, after only a few moments.

Then they lay in each other's arms, dozing until the urge took over them again. They made love slower this time, at a less intense pace but with no less desire than before.

****

Ivy awoke a few hours later and looked over at Lucas. She couldn't believe they had found their way back to each other. He looked so relaxed in sleep—not the stressed out lost boy she had seen in Central Park.

She wanted to let him rest, so she quietly slipped out of bed and into the bathroom. It was beautifully appointed with gray marble countertops and white fixtures. There was a large glass shower with a fancy LED shower head. She turned on the luxurious tap and stepped inside. The warm spray and steam, accompanied by the soft light, relaxed her even more if that were possible. She was just reaching for the shampoo when strong, warm arms encircled her waist from behind.

"Hey," Lucas murmured in her ear. "You left me."

She smiled and leaned against his strong chest. Then she handed him the bottle. "You were sleeping, and I know you need your rest."

"What I need is you," he said and put the bottle aside. Then he spun her around and kissed her with so much devotion, she lost all sense of time and reason.

A half hour later, Ivy was dressed in pink pajama shorts and a camisole, and they were sitting at the table in their suite. Lucas had put on some black lounging pants, but he remained bare-chested, and Ivy was enjoying the view of his muscular torso.

They had been talking for a while, and Lucas had told her the whole story. Ivy was stunned, but extremely elated, everything had turned out. She cried tears of joy when Lucas told her Ben and Karen would be adopting baby Ryan. Lucas told her he called the adoption lawyer to thank him, and he mentioned Deanna had taken a plane back to Kentucky. She said she was going to try and start over with the help of her hometown family and friends. Everyone, it seemed, was getting a happy ending.

Lucas's voice roused her from her wayward thoughts. "I ordered this dinner for us to have hours ago. Good thing everything was on ice. Are you hungry?"

"Yes, very," Ivy said. "But hey, aren't a newly engaged couple supposed to toast with champagne? I see it there, but my fiancé has yet to pour me a glass."

He looked up at her with his stunning green eyes. His smile was genuine and full. "Well, it was ready for you hours ago, but you had something else in mind to celebrate our engagement."

"Yes, well that was then," she said with a wicked gleam in her eye. "Now I want champagne."

"As you wish, my soon-to-be Mrs. Freeman." He scooped her up and sat her down gently in the chair. Then he reached for the expensive Rosé chilling in an ice bucket. He popped the cork and poured them each a flute.

He handed her one, his eyes never leaving hers, and she saw all the love he had for her in his tender expression. She accepted the glass and he said to her, "To what would you like to toast?"

"Us," she replied. "Because from this moment on,

Lucas, I promise you that we will walk together, hand in hand, wherever our journey leads us—until the end of time."

She held up her glass to his, and they clinked together in a soft, chiming sound.

"To us," he said back to her. "And I promise you, Ivy, I will dedicate myself to you. Nothing and no one can separate us now. We will grow old together and love each other with all of the passion I feel right here and now—forever."

They sipped their champagne, entwined in each other's arms, and Ivy realized all the dreams she had been holding on to for so long were finally taking flight.

A word about the author...

After writing more essays than she could count completing her university studies, Kate Randle decided to swap out the world of academic prose for something more exciting—romance novels.

She lives near Toronto, Ontario, with her incredibly supportive husband and kids. Two adorable felines round out her family to keep things interesting and covered in cat hair.

For more information, please visit Kate at her website: www.katerandle.com